HORNBLOWER GOES TO SEA

Horatio Hornblower, R.N., is the best-known and best-loved sailor in modern fiction. The story of his life, from the inexperienced midshipman (who had the indelicacy to be seasick while riding at anchor in Spithead) to the dauntless Captain who almost single handed captured a French gun emplacement on enemy territory, has held thousands of readers enthralled since the first book was published nearly fifty years ago.

For Hornblower not only manages to get involved in every adventure available to men fighting at sea during the epoch of Lord Nelson, but the men and women he encounters on his way are fascinating human beings drawn by the hand of a master novelist.

This specially edited edition, first published in 1954, includes many of the most exciting exploits which occurred in the pages of *Mr Midshipman Hornblower* and *Lieutenant Hornblower*.

C. S. Forester was born in Cairo in 1899. He studied medicine at Guy's Hospital, London, and then turned to writing as a career. In 1932 he was offered a Hollywood contract, and from then until 1939 he spent thirteen weeks of every year in America. During the war he entered the Ministry of Information and later served with the Royal Navy. In Hornblower he created the most renowned sailor in contemporary fiction. Forester died in 1966.

Soames standing up in the sternsheets looking at the death which was cleaving the blue water

C. S. FORESTER

HORNBLOWER
GOES TO SEA

SELECTED BY G. P. GRIGGS

ILLUSTRATIONS BY
GEOFFREY WHITTAM

PUFFIN BOOKS

Puffin Books, Penguin Books Ltd, Harmondsworth, Middlesex, England
Viking Penguin Inc., 40 West 23rd Street, New York, New York 10010, U.S.A.
Penguin Books Australia Ltd, Ringwood, Victoria, Australia
Penguin Books Canada Ltd, 2801 John Street, Markham, Ontario, Canada L3R 1B4
Penguin Books (N.Z.) Ltd, 182–190 Wairau Road, Auckland 10, New Zealand

—

First published by Michael Joseph 1954
Published in Peacock Books 1963
Reprinted 1965, 1969
Reissued in Puffin Books 1972
Reprinted 1973, 1975, 1985

—

—

Printed and bound in Great Britain by
Cox & Wyman Ltd, Reading
Set in Monotype Imprint

Contents

The Even Chance

A JANUARY gale was roaring up the Channel, bluster-
ing loudly, and bearing in its bosom rain squalls
whose big drops rattled loudly on the tarpaulin
clothing of those among the officers and men whose duties
kept them on deck. So hard and so long had the gale
blown that even in the sheltered waters of Spithead the
battleship moved uneasily at her anchors, pitching a little
in the choppy seas, and snubbing herself against the
tauntened cables with unexpected jerks. A shore boat was
on its way out to her, propelled by oars in the hands of
two sturdy women; it danced madly on the steep little
waves, now and then putting its nose into one and sending
a sheet of spray flying aft. The oarswoman in the bow
knew her business, and with rapid glances over her
shoulder not only kept the boat on its course but turned
the bows into the worst of the waves to keep from cap-
sizing. It slowly drew up along the starboard side of the
Justinian, and as it approached the main-chains the midshipman of the watch hailed it.

'Aye aye' came back the answering hail from the lusty
lungs of the woman at the stroke oar; by the curious and
ages-old convention of the Navy the reply meant that the
boat had an officer on board – presumably the huddled
figure in the sternsheets looking more like a heap of trash
with a boat-cloak thrown over it.

That was as much as Mr Masters, the lieutenant of the
watch, could see; he was sheltering as best he could in
the lee of the mizen-mast bitts, and in obedience to the
order of the midshipman of the watch the boat drew up

towards the main-chains and passed out of his sight. There was a long delay; apparently the officer had some difficulty in getting up the ship's side. At last the boat reappeared in Masters's field of vision; the women had shoved off and were setting a scrap of lugsail, under which the boat, now without its passenger, went swooping back towards Portsmouth, leaping on the waves like a steeplechaser. As it departed Mr Masters became aware of the near approach of someone along the quarter-deck; it was the new arrival under the escort of the midshipman of the watch.

He looked with attention at the approaching figure. It was that of a skinny young man only just leaving boyhood behind, something above middle height, with feet whose adolescent proportions to his size were accentuated by the thinness of his legs and his big half-boots. His gawkiness called attention to his hands and elbows. The new-comer was dressed in a badly-fitting uniform which was soaked right through by the spray; a skinny neck stuck out of the high stock, and above the neck was a white, bony face. A white face was a rarity on the deck of a ship of war, whose crew soon tanned to a deep mahogany, but this face was not merely white; in the hollow cheeks there was a faint shade of green – clearly the newcomer had experienced seasickness in his passage out in the shore boat. Set in the white face were a pair of dark eyes which by contrast looked like holes cut in a sheet of paper; Masters noted with a slight stirring of interest that the eyes, despite their owner's seasickness, were looking about keenly, taking in what were obviously new sights; there was a curiosity and interest there which could not be repressed and which continued to function notwithstanding either seasickness or shyness.

The dark eyes met Masters's, and the gawky figure came

to a halt, raising a hand self-consciously to the brim of his dripping hat. His mouth opened and tried to say something, but closed again without achieving its object as shyness overcame him, but then the new-comer nerved himself afresh and forced himself to say the formal words he had been coached to utter.

'Come aboard, sir.'

'Your name?' asked Masters, after waiting for it for a moment.

'H-Horatio Hornblower, sir. Midshipman,' stuttered the boy.

'Very good, Mr Hornblower,' said Masters, with the equally formal response. 'Did you bring your dunnage aboard with you?'

Hornblower had never heard that word before, but he still had enough of his wits about him to deduce what it meant.

'My sea chest, sir. It's – it's forrard, at the entry port.'

Hornblower said these things with the barest hesitation; he knew that at sea they said them, that they pronounced the word 'forward' like that, and that he had come on board through the 'entry port', but it called for a slight effort to utter them himself.

'I'll see that it's sent below,' said Masters. 'And that's where you'd better go, too. The captain's ashore, and the first lieutenant's orders were that he's not to be called on any account before eight bells, so I advise you, Mr Hornblower, to get out of those wet clothes while you can.'

'Aye aye, sir,' said Hornblower, and as an afterthought he put his hand to the brim of his hat again.

Master returned the compliment and turned to one of the shivering messengers cowering in the inadequate shelter of the bulwark. 'Boy! Take Mr Hornblower down to the midshipman's berth.'

'Aye aye, sir.'

Hornblower accompanied the boy forward to the main hatchway. Seasickness alone would have made him unsteady on his feet, but twice on the short journey he stumbled like a man tripping over a rope as a sharp gust brought the *Justinian* up against her cables with a jerk. At the hatchway the boy slid down the ladder like an eel over a rock; Hornblower had to brace himself and descend far more gingerly and uncertainly into the dim light of the lower gundeck and then into the twilight of the 'tweendecks. The smells that entered his nostrils were as strange and as assorted as the noises that assailed his ears. At the foot of each ladder the boy waited for him with a patience whose tolerance was just obvious. After the last descent, a few steps – Hornblower had already lost his sense of direction and did not know whether it was aft or forward – took them to a gloomy recess whose shadows were accentuated rather than lightened by a tallow dip spiked on to a bit of copper plate on a table round which were seated half a dozen shirt-sleeved men. The boy vanished and left Hornblower standing there, and it was a second or two before the whiskered man at the head of the table looked up at him.

'Speak, thou apparition,' said he.

Hornblower felt a wave of nausea overcoming him – the after effects of his trip in the shore boat were being accentuated by the incredible stuffiness and smelliness of the 'tweendecks. It was very hard to speak, and the fact that he did not know how to phrase what he wanted to say made it harder still.

'My name is Hornblower,' he quavered at length.

'What an infernal piece of bad luck for you,' said a second man at the table, with a complete absence of sympathy.

At that moment in the roaring world outside the ship the wind veered sharply, heeling the *Justinian* a trifle and swinging her round to snub at her cables again. To Hornblower it seemed more as if the world had come loose from its fastenings. He reeled where he stood, and although he was shuddering with cold he felt sweat on his face.

'I suppose you have come,' said the whiskered man at the head of the table, 'to thrust yourself among your betters. Another soft-headed ignoramus come to be a nuisance to those who have to try to teach you your duties. Look at him' – the speaker, with a gesture, demanded the attention of everyone at the table – 'look at him, I say! The King's latest bad bargain. How old are you?'

'S-seventeen, sir,' stuttered Hornblower.

'Seventeen!' the disgust in the speaker's voice was only too evident. 'You must start at twelve if you ever wish to be a seaman.'

The ship lurched again at that moment, and he clung on to the table.

'Gentlemen,' he began pathetically, wondering how to say what he had in mind.

'My God!' exclaimed somebody at the table. 'He's seasick!'

'Seasick in Spithead!' said somebody else, in a tone in which amazement had as much place as disgust.

But Hornblower ceased to care; he was not really conscious of what was going on round him for some time after that. The nervous excitement of the last few days was as much to blame, perhaps, as the journey in the shore boat and the erratic behaviour of the *Justinian* at her anchors, but it meant for him that he was labelled at once as the midshipman who was seasick in Spithead, and it was only natural that the label added to the natural misery of the loneliness and home-sickness which oppressed him during those days when that part of the Channel Fleet which had not succeeded in completing its crews lay at anchor in the lee of the Isle of Wight. An hour in the hammock into which the messman hoisted him enabled him to recover sufficiently to be able to report himself to the first lieutenant; after a few days on board he was able to find his way round the ship without losing his sense of direction below decks. During that period his brother officers ceased to have faces which were mere blurs and came to take on personalities; he came painfully to learn the stations allotted him when the ship was at quarters, when he was on watch, and when hands were summoned for setting or taking in sail. He even came to have an acute enough understanding of his new life to realize that it could have been worse – that destiny might have put him on board a ship ordered immediately to sea instead of one lying at anchor. But it was a poor enough compensation; he was a lonely and unhappy boy. Shyness alone would long have delayed his making friends, but as it happened the midshipman's berth in the *Justinian* was occupied by men all a good deal older than he. They were inclined, after the first moments of amused interest, to ignore him, and he was glad of it, delighted to shrink into his shell and attract no notice to himself.

For the *Justinian* was not a happy ship during those gloomy January days. Captain Keene was a sick man, of a melancholy disposition. His officers saw little of him, and did not love what they saw. Hornblower, summoned to his cabin for his first interview, was not impressed – a middle-aged man at a table covered with papers, with the hollow and yellow cheeks of prolonged illness.

'Mr Hornblower,' he said formally, 'I am glad to have this opportunity of welcoming you on board my ship.'

'Yes, sir,' said Hornblower – that seemed more appropriate to the occasion than 'Aye aye, sir', and a junior midshipman seemed to be expected to say one or the other on all occasions.

'You are – let me see – seventeen?' Captain Keene picked up the paper which apparently covered Hornblower's brief official career.

'Yes, sir.'

'July 4th, 1776,' mused Keene, reading Hornblower's date of birth to himself. 'A doctor's son – you should have chosen a lord for your father if you wanted to make a career for yourself.'

'Yes, sir.'

'How far did your education go?'

'I was a Grecian at school, sir.'

'So you can construe Xenophon as well as Cicero?'

'Yes, sir. But not very well, sir.'

'Better if you knew something about sines and cosines. Better if you could foresee a squall in time to get t'gallants in. We have no use for ablative absolutes in the Navy.'

'Yes, sir,' said Hornblower.

'Well, obey orders, learn your duties, and no harm can come to you. That will do.'

'Thank you, sir,' said Hornblower, retiring.

But the captain's last words to him seemed to be contradicted immediately. Harm began to come to Hornblower from that day forth, despite his obedience to orders and diligent study of his duties, and it stemmed from the arrival in the midshipmen's berth of John Simpson as senior warrant officer. Hornblower was sitting at mess with his colleagues when he first saw him – a brawny, good-looking man in his thirties, who came in and stood looking at them just as Hornblower had stood a few days before.

'Hullo!' said somebody, not very cordially.

'Cleveland, my bold friend,' said the new-comer, 'come out from that seat. I am going to resume my place at the head of the table.'

'But – '

'Come out, I said,' snapped Simpson.

Cleveland moved along with some show of reluctance, and Simpson took his place, and glowered round the table in reply to the curious glances with which everyone regarded him.

'Yes, my sweet brother officers,' he said, 'I am back in the bosom of the family. And I am not surprised that nobody is pleased. You will all be less pleased by the time I am done with you, I may add.'

'But your commission – ?' asked somebody, greatly daring.

'My commission?' Simpson leaned forward and tapped the table, staring down the inquisitive people on either side of it. 'I'll answer that question this once, and the man who asks it again will wish he had never been born. A board of turnip-headed captains has refused me my commission. It decided that my mathematical knowledge was insufficient to make me a reliable navigator. And so Acting-Lieutenant Simpson is once again Mr Midshipman Simpson, at your service. At your service. And may the Lord have mercy on your souls.'

It did not seem, as the days went by, that the Lord had any mercy at all, for with Simpson's return life in the midshipmen's berth ceased to be one of passive unhappiness and became one of active misery. Simpson had apparently always been an ingenious tyrant, but now, embittered and humiliated by his failure to pass his examination for his commission, he was a worse tyrant, and his ingenuity had multiplied itself. He may have been weak in mathematics, but he was diabolically clever at making other people's lives a burden to them. As senior officer in the mess he had wide official powers; as a man with a blistering tongue and a morbid sense of mischief he would have been powerful anyway, even if the *Justinian* had possessed an alert and masterful first lieutenant to keep him in check, while Mr Clay was neither. Twice midshipmen rebelled against Simpson's arbitrary authority, and each time Simpson thrashed the rebel, pounding him into insensibility with his huge fists, for Simpson would have made a successful prize-fighter. Each time Simpson was left unmarked; each time his opponent's blackened eyes and swollen lips called down the penalty of mast-heading and extra duty from the indignant first lieutenant. The mess seethed with impotent rage. Even the toadies and lickspittles among the midshipmen – and naturally there were several – hated the tyrant.

Significantly, it was not his ordinary exactions which roused the greatest resentment – his levying toll upon their sea chests for clean shirts for himself, his appropriation of the best cuts of the meat served, nor even his taking their coveted issues of spirits. These things could be excused as understandable, the sort of thing they would do themselves if they had the power. But he displayed a whimsical arbitrariness which reminded Hornblower, with his classical education, of the freaks of the Roman emperors. He forced Cleveland to shave the whiskers which were his inordinate pride; he imposed upon Hether the duty of waking up Mackenzie every half-hour, day and night, so that neither of them was able to sleep – and there were toadies ready to tell him if Hether ever failed in his task. Early enough he had discovered Hornblower's most vulnerable points, as he had with everyone else. He knew of Hornblower's shyness; at first it was amusing to compel Hornblower to recite verses from Gray's 'Elegy in a Country Churchyard' to the assembled mess. The toadies could compel Hornblower to do it; Simpson would lay his dirk-scabbard on the table in front of him with a significant glance, and the toadies would close round Hornblower, who knew that any hesitation on his part would mean that he would be stretched across the table and the dirk-scabbard applied; the flat of the scabbard was painful, the edge of it was agonizing, but the pain was nothing to the utter humiliation of it all. And the torment grew worse when Simpson instituted what he aptly called 'The Proceedings of the Inquisition', when Hornblower was submitted to a slow and methodical questioning regarding his home life and his boyhood. Every question had to be answered on pain of the dirk-scabbard; Hornblower could fence and prevaricate, but he had to answer and sooner or later the relentless questioning would draw from him some simple admission which would rouse a peal of laughter from his audience. Heaven knows that in Hornblower's lonely childhood there was nothing to be ashamed of, but boys are odd creatures, especially reticent ones like Hornblower, and are ashamed of things no one else would think twice about. The ordeal would leave him weak and sick; someone less solemn might have clowned his way out of his difficulties and even into popular favour, but Hornblower at seventeen was too ponderous a person to clown. He never wept in public, but at night more than once he shed the bitter tears of seventeen. He often thought about death; he often even thought about desertion, but he realized that desertion would lead to something worse than death, and then his mind would revert to death, savouring the thought of suicide.

If the ship had only been at sea everyone would have

been kept busy enough to be out of mischief; even at anchor an energetic captain and first lieutenant would have kept all hands hard enough at work to obviate abuses, but it was Hornblower's hard luck that the *Justinian* lay at anchor all through that fatal January of 1794 under a sick captain and an inefficient first lieutenant. Even the activities which were at times enforced often worked to Hornblower's disadvantage. There was an occasion when Mr Bowles, the master, was holding a class in navigation for his mates and for the midshipmen, and the captain by bad luck happened by and glanced through the results of the problem the class had individually been set to solve. His illness made Keene a man of bitter tongue, and he cherished no liking for Simpson. He took a single glance at Simpson's paper, and chuckled sarcastically.

'Now let us all rejoice,' he said, 'the sources of the Nile have been discovered at last.'

'Pardon, sir?' said Simpson.

'Your ship,' said Keene, 'as far as I can make out from your illiterate scrawl, Mr Simpson, is in Central Africa. Let us now see what other *terrae incognitae* have been opened up by the remaining intrepid explorers of this class.'

It must have been Fate – it was dramatic enough to be art and not an occurrence in real life; Hornblower knew what was going to happen even as Keene picked up the other papers, including his. The result he had obtained was the only one which was correct; everybody else had added the correction for refraction instead of subtracting it, or had worked out the multiplication wrongly, or had, like Simpson, botched the whole problem.

'Congratulations, Mr Hornblower,' said Keene. 'You must be proud to be alone successful among this crowd of intellectual giants. You are half Mr Simpson's age, I fancy. If you double your attainments while you double your years, you will leave the rest of us far behind. Mr Bowles, you will be so good as to see that Mr Simpson pays even further attention to his mathematical studies.'

With that he went off along the 'tweendecks with the halting step resulting from his mortal disease, and Hornblower sat with his eyes cast down, unable to meet the glances he knew were being darted at him, and knowing full well what they portended. He longed for death at that moment; he even prayed for it that night.

Within two days Hornblower found himself on shore, and under Simpson's command. The two midshipmen were in charge of a party of seamen, landed to act along with parties from the other ships of the squadron as a press gang. The West India convoy was due to arrive soon; most of the hands would be pressed as soon as the convoy reached the Channel, and the remainder, left to work the ships to an anchorage, would sneak ashore, using every device to conceal themselves and find a safe hiding-place. It was the business of the landing parties to cut off this retreat, to lay a cordon along the water-front which would sweep them all up. But the convoy was not yet signalled, and all arrangements were completed.

'All is well with the world,' said Simpson.

It was an unusual speech for him, but he was in unusual circumstances. He was sitting in the back room of the Lamb Inn, comfortable in one arm-chair with his legs on another, in front of a roaring fire and with a pot of beer with gin in it at his elbow.

'Here's to the West India convoy,' said Simpson, taking a pull at his beer. 'Long may it be delayed.'

Simpson was actually genial, activity and beer and a warm fire thawing him into a good humour; it was not time yet for the liquor to make him quarrelsome; Hornblower sat on the other side of the fire and sipped beer without gin in it and studied him, marvelling that for the first time since he had boarded the *Justinian* his un-happiness should have ceased to be active but should have subsided into a dull misery like the dying away of the pain of a throbbing tooth.

'Give us a toast, boy,' said Simpson.

'Confusion to Robespierre,' said Hornblower lamely.

The door opened and two more officers came in, one a midshipman while the other wore the single epaulette of a lieutenant – it was Chalk of the *Goliath*, the officer in general charge of the press gangs sent ashore. Even Simpson made room for his superior rank before the fire.

'The convoy is still not signalled,' announced Chalk. And then he eyed Hornblower keenly. 'I don't think I have the pleasure of your acquaintance.'

'Mr Hornblower – Lieutenant Chalk,' introduced Simpson. 'Mr Hornblower is distinguished as the mid-shipman who was seasick in Spithead.'

Hornblower tried not to writhe as Simpson tied that label on him. He imagined that Chalk was merely being polite when he changed the subject.

'Hey, potman! Will you gentlemen join me in a glass? We have a long wait before us, I fear. Your men are all properly posted, Mr Simpson?'

'Yes, sir.'

Chalk was an active man. He paced about the room, stared out of the window at the rain, presented his mid-shipman – Caldwell – to the other two when the drinks arrived, and obviously fretted at his enforced inactivity.

'A game of cards to pass the time?' he suggested. 'Excellent! Hey, potman! Cards and a table and another light.'

The table was set before the fire, the chairs arranged, the cards brought in.

'What game shall it be?' asked Chalk, looking round.

He was a lieutenant among three midshipmen, and any suggestion of his was likely to carry a good deal of weight; the other three naturally waited to hear what he had to say.

'Vingt-et-un? That is a game for the half-witted. Loo? That is a game for the wealthier half-witted. But whist, now? That would give us all scope for the exercise of our poor talents. Caldwell, there, is acquainted with the rudiments of the game, I know. Mr Simpson?'

A man like Simpson, with a blind mathematical spot, was not likely to be a good whist player, but he was not likely to know he was a bad one.

'As you wish, sir,' said Simpson. He enjoyed gambling, and one game was as good as another for that purpose to his mind.

'Mr Hornblower?'

'With pleasure, sir.'

That was more nearly true than most conventional replies. Hornblower had learned his whist in a good school; ever since the death of his mother he had made a fourth with his father and the parson and the parson's wife. The game was already something of a passion with him. He revelled in the nice calculation of chances, in the varying demands it made upon his boldness or caution. There was even enough warmth in his acceptance to attract a second glance from Chalk, who – a good card player himself – at once detected a fellow spirit.

'Excellent!' he said again. 'Then we may as well cut at once for places and partners. What shall be the stakes, gentlemen? A shilling a trick and a guinea on the rub, or is that too great? No? Then we are agreed.'

For some time the game proceeded quietly. Hornblower

cut first Simpson and then Caldwell as his partner. Only a couple of hands were necessary to show up Simpson as a hopeless whist player, but he and Hornblower won the first rubber, thanks to overwhelming card strength. But Simpson lost the next in partnership with Chalk, cut Chalk again as partner, and lost again. As his losses grew, and as the potman came and went with liquor, he grew restless, and his face was flushed with more than the heat of the fire. He was both a bad loser and a bad drinker, and even Chalk's punctilious good manners were sufficiently strained so that he displayed a hint of relief when the next cut gave him Hornblower as a partner. They won the rubber easily, and another guinea and several shillings were transferred to Hornblower's lean purse; he was now the only winner, and Simpson was the heaviest loser. Hornblower was lost in the pleasure of playing the game again; the only attention he paid to Simpson's writhings and muttered objurgations was to regard them as a distracting nuisance; he even forgot to think of them as danger signals. Momentarily he was oblivious to the fact that he might pay for his present success by future torment.

Once more they cut, and he found himself Chalk's partner again. Two good hands gave them the first game and, as they neared the end of the next, and seeing that the remaining tricks were his, Hornblower laid down his cards.

'The rest are mine,' he said.

'What do you mean?' said Simpson, who still had the king of diamonds in his hand.

'Five tricks,' said Chalk briskly. 'Game and rubber.'

'But don't I take another?' persisted Simpson.

'I trump a lead of diamonds or hearts and make three more clubs,' explained Hornblower. To him the situation was as simple as two and two, a most ordinary finish to a hand; it was hard for him to realize that foggy-minded players like Simpson could find difficulty in keeping tally of fifty-two cards. Simpson flung down his hand.

'You know too much about the game,' he said. 'You know the backs of the cards as well as the fronts.'

Hornblower gulped. He recognized that this could be a decisive moment if he chose. A second before he had merely been playing cards, and enjoying himself. Now he was faced with an issue of life or death. A torrent of thought streamed through his mind. Despite the comfort of his present surroundings he remembered acutely the hideous misery of the life in the *Justinian* to which he must return. This was an opportunity to end that misery one way or the other. He remembered how he had contemplated killing himself, and into the back of his mind stole the germ of the plan upon which he was going to act. His decision crystallized.

'That is an insulting remark, Mr Simpson,' he said. He looked round and met the eyes of Chalk and Caldwell, who were suddenly grave; Simpson was still merely stupid. 'For that I shall have to ask satisfaction.'

'Satisfaction?' said Chalk hastily. 'Come, come. Mr Simpson had a momentary loss of temper. I am sure he will explain.'

'I have been accused of cheating at cards,' said Hornblower. 'That's a hard thing to explain away.'

He was trying to behave like a grown man; more than that, he was trying to act like a man consumed with indignation, while actually there was no indignation within him over the point in dispute, for he understood too well the muddled state of mind which had led Simpson to say what he did. But the opportunity had presented itself, he had determined to avail himself of it, and now

22

what he had to do was to play the part convincingly of the man who has received a mortal insult.

'The wine was in and the wit was out,' said Chalk, still determined on keeping the peace. 'Mr Simpson was speaking in jest, I am sure. Let's call for another bottle and drink it in friendship.'

'With pleasure,' said Hornblower, fumbling for the words which would set the dispute beyond reconciliation. 'If Mr Simpson will beg my pardon at once before you two gentlemen, and admit that he spoke without justification and in a manner no gentleman would employ.'

He turned and met Simpson's eyes with defiance as he spoke, metaphorically waving a red rag before the bull, who charged with gratifying fury.

'Apologize to *you*, you little whippersnapper!' exploded Simpson, alcohol and outraged dignity speaking simultaneously. 'Never this side of Hell.'

'You hear that, gentlemen?' said Hornblower. 'I have been insulted and Mr Simpson refuses to apologize while insulting me further. There is only one way now in which satisfaction can be given.'

For the next two days, until the West India convoy came in, Hornblower and Simpson, under Chalk's orders, lived the curious life of two duellists forced into each other's society before the affair of honour. Hornblower was careful – as he would have been in any case – to obey every order given him, and Simpson gave them with a certain amount of self-consciousness and awkwardness. It was during those two days that Hornblower elaborated on his original idea.

He first brought forward his suggestion in conversation with Preston and Danvers, the two master's mates whom he asked to be his seconds as soon as he returned to the *Justinian*.

'We'll act for you, of course,' said Preston, looking dubiously at the weedy youth when he made his request. 'How do you want to fight him? As the aggrieved party you have the choice of weapons.'

'I've been thinking about it ever since he insulted me,' said Hornblower temporizing. It was not easy to come out with his idea in bald words, after all.

'Have you any skill with the small-sword?' asked Danvers.

'No,' said Hornblower. Truth to tell, he had never even handled one.

'Then it had better be pistols,' said Preston.

'Simpson is probably a good shot,' said Danvers. 'I wouldn't care to stand up before him myself.'

'Easy now,' said Preston hastily. 'Don't dishearten the man.'

'I'm not disheartened,' said Hornblower, 'I was thinking the same thing myself.'

'You're cool enough about it, then,' marvelled Danvers. Hornblower shrugged.

'Maybe I am. I hardly care. But I've thought that we might make the chances more even.'

'How?'

'We could make them exactly even,' said Hornblower, taking the plunge. 'Have two pistols, one loaded and the other empty. Simpson and I would take our choice without knowing which was which. Then we stand within a yard of each other, and at the word we fire.'

'My God!' said Danvers.

'I don't think that would be legal,' said Preston. 'It would mean one of you would be killed for certain.'

'Killing is the object of duelling,' said Hornblower. 'If the conditions aren't unfair I don't think any objection can be raised.'

'But would you carry it out to the end?' marvelled Danvers.

'Mr Danvers – ' began Hornblower; but Preston interfered.

'We won't want another duel on our hands,' he said. 'Danvers only meant he wouldn't care to do it himself. We'll discuss it with Cleveland and Hether, and see what they say.'

Within an hour the proposed conditions of the duel were known to everyone in the ship. Perhaps it was to Simpson's disadvantage that he had no real friend in the ship, for Cleveland and Hether, his seconds, were not disposed to take too firm a stand regarding the conditions of the duel, and agreed to the terms with only a show of reluctance. At noon Lieutenant Masters sent for Hornblower.

'The captain has ordered me to make inquiry into this duel, Mr Hornblower,' he said. 'I am instructed to use my best endeavours to compose the quarrel.'

'Yes, sir.'

'Why insist on this satisfaction, Mr Hornblower? I understand there were a few hasty words over wine and cards.'

'Mr Simpson accused me of cheating, sir, before witnesses who were not officers of this ship.'

'Even so, there can be satisfaction without a duel, Mr Hornblower.'

'If Mr Simpson will make me a full apology before the same gentlemen, I would be satisfied, sir.'

Simpson was no coward. He would die rather than submit to such a formal humiliation.

'I see. Now I understand you are insisting on rather unusual conditions for the duel?'

'There are precedents for it, sir. As the insulted party I can choose any conditions which are not unfair.'

'You sound like a sea lawyer to me, Mr Hornblower.'

The hint was sufficient to tell Hornblower that he had verged upon being too glib, and he resolved in future to bridle his tongue. He stood silent and waited for Masters to resume the conversation.

'You are determined, then, Mr Hornblower, to continue with this murderous business?'

'Yes, sir.'

'The captain has given me further orders to attend the duel in person, because of the strange conditions on which you insist. I must inform you that I shall request the seconds to arrange for that.'

'Yes, sir.'

'Very good, then, Mr Hornblower.'

Masters looked at Hornblower as he dismissed him even more keenly than he had done when Hornblower first came on board. He was looking for signs of weakness or wavering -- indeed, he was looking for any signs of human feeling at all -- but he could detect none. Hornblower had reached a decision, he had weighed all the pros and cons, and his logical mind told him that having decided in cold blood upon a course of action it would be folly to allow himself to be influenced subsequently by untrustworthy emotions. The conditions of the duel on which he was insisting were mathematically advantageous. If he had once considered with favour escaping from Simpson's persecution by a voluntary death it was surely a gain to take an even chance of escaping from it without dying. Similarly, if Simpson were (as he almost certainly was) a better swordsman and a better pistol shot than him, the even chance was again mathematically advantageous. There was nothing to regret about his recent actions.

All very well; mathematically the conclusions were irrefutable, but Hornblower was surprised to find that mathematics were not everything. Repeatedly during that dreary afternoon and evening Hornblower found himself suddenly gulping with anxiety as the realization came to him afresh that tomorrow morning he would be risking his life on the spin of a coin. The thought sent a shiver through him despite himself. He slung his hammock that night in a depressed mood, feeling unnaturally tired; and he undressed in the clammy, stuffy dampness of the 'tweendecks feeling more than usually cold. He hugged the blankets round himself, yearning to relax in their warmth, but relaxation would not come. He turned over wearily a dozen times, hearing the ship's bell ring out each half hour, feeling a growing contempt at his cowardice. He told himself in the end that it was as well that his fate tomorrow depended upon pure chance, for if he had to rely upon steadiness of hand and eye he would be dead for certain after a night like this.

That conclusion presumably helped him to go to sleep for the last hour or two of the night, for he awoke with a start to find Danvers shaking him.

'Five bells,' said Danvers. 'Dawn in an hour. Rise and shine!'

Hornblower slid out of his hammock and stood in his shirt; the 'tweendecks was nearly dark and Danvers was almost invisible.

'Number One's letting us have the second cutter,' said Danvers. 'Masters and Simpson and that lot are going first in the launch. Here's Preston.'

Another shadowy figure loomed up in the darkness.

'Hellish cold,' said Preston. 'The devil of a morning to turn out. Nelson, where's that tea?'

The mess attendant came with it as Hornblower was hauling on his trousers. It maddened Hornblower that he shivered enough in the cold for the cup to clatter in the saucer as he took it, but he drank the tea eagerly.

'Give me another cup,' he said, and was proud of himself that he could think about tea at that moment.

It was still dark as they went down into the cutter. There was a keen, cold wind blowing which filled the dipping lug as the boat headed for the twin lights that marked the jetty.

'I ordered a hackney coach at the *George* to be waiting for us,' said Danvers. 'Let's hope it is.'

It was, and Danvers produced a pocket flask as they settled themselves in with their feet in the straw.

'Take a sip, Hornblower?' he asked. 'There's no special need for a steady hand this morning.'

'No thank you,' said Hornblower. His empty stomach revolted at the idea of pouring spirits into it.

The hackney coach levelled itself off as it came over the crest of the hill, and stopped beside the common. Another coach stood there waiting, its single candle-lamp burning yellow in the growing dawn.

'There they are,' said Preston; the faint light revealed a shadowy group standing on frosty turf among the gorse bushes.

Hornblower, as they approached, caught a glimpse of Simpson's face as he stood a little detached from the others. It was pale, and Hornblower noticed that at that moment he swallowed nervously, just as he himself was doing. Masters came towards them, shooting his usual keen inquisitive look at Hornblower as they came together.

'This is the moment,' he said, 'for this quarrel to be composed. This country is at war. I hope, Mr Hornblower, that you can be persuaded to save a life for the King's service by not pressing this matter.'

Hornblower looked across at Simpson, while Danvers answered for him.

'Has Mr Simpson offered the proper redress?' asked Danvers.

'Mr Simpson is willing to acknowledge that he wishes the incident had never taken place.'

'That is an unsatisfactory form,' said Danvers. 'It does not include an apology, and you must agree that an apology is necessary, sir.'

'What does your principal say?' persisted Masters.

'It is not for any principal to speak in these circumstances,' said Danvers, with a glance at Hornblower, who nodded. All this was as inevitable as the ride in the hangman's cart, and as hideous. There could be no going back now; Hornblower had never thought for one moment that Simpson would apologize, and without an apology the affair must be carried to a bloody conclusion. An even chance that he did not have five minutes longer to live.

'You are determined, then, gentlemen,' said Masters. 'I shall have to state that fact in my report.'

'We are determined,' said Preston.

'Then there is nothing for it but to allow this deplorable affair to proceed. I left the pistols in charge of Doctor Hepplewhite.'

He turned and led them towards the other group – Simpson with Hether and Cleveland, and Doctor Hepplewhite standing with a pistol held by the muzzle in each hand. He was a bulky man with the red face of a persistent drinker; he was actually grinning a spirituous grin at that moment, rocking a little on his feet.

'Are the young fools set in their folly?' he asked; but everyone very properly ignored him as having no business to ask such a question at such a moment.

'Now,' said Masters. 'Here are the pistols, both primed, as you see, but one loaded and the other unloaded, in accordance with the conditions. I have here a guinea which I propose to spin to decide the allocation of the weapons. Now, gentlemen, shall the spin give your principals one pistol each irrevocably – for instance, if the coin shows heads shall Mr Simpson have this one – or shall the winner of the spin have choice of weapons? It is my design to eliminate all possibility of collusion as far as possible.'

Hether and Cleveland and Danvers and Preston exchanged dubious glances.

'Let the winner of the spin choose,' said Preston at length.

'Very well, gentlemen. Please call, Mr Hornblower.'

'Tails!' said Hornblower as the gold piece spun in the air.

Masters caught it and clapped a hand over it.

'Tails it is,' said Masters, lifting his hand and revealing the coin to the grouped seconds. 'Please make your choice.'

Hepplewhite held out the two pistols to him, death in one hand and life in the other. It was a grim moment. There was only pure chance to direct him; it called for a little effort to force his hand out.

'I'll have this one,' he said; as he touched it the weapon seemed icy cold.

'Then now I have done what was required of me,' said Masters. 'The rest is for you gentlemen to carry out.'

'Take this one, Simpson,' said Hepplewhite. 'And be careful how you handle yours, Mr Hornblower. You're a public danger.'

The man was still grinning, gloating over the fact that someone else was in mortal danger while he himself was in none. Simpson took the pistol Hepplewhite offered him and settled it into his hand; once more his eyes met Hornblower's, but there was neither recognition nor expression in them.

'There are no distances to step out,' Danvers was saying. 'One spot's as good as another. It's level enough here.'

'Very good,' said Hether. 'Will you stand here, Mr Simpson?'

Preston beckoned to Hornblower, who walked over. It was not easy to appear brisk and unconcerned. Preston took him by the arm and stood up in front of Simpson, almost breast to breast – close enough to smell the alcohol on his breath.

'For the last time, gentlemen,' said Masters loudly, 'cannot you be reconciled?'

There was no answer from anybody, only deep silence, during which it seemed to Hornblower that the frantic beating of his heart must be clearly audible. The silence was broken by an exclamation from Hether.

'We haven't settled who's to give the word!' he said. 'Who's going to?'

'Let's ask Mr Masters to give it,' said Danvers.

Hornblower did not look round. He was looking steadfastly at the grey sky past Simpson's right ear – somehow he could not look him in the face, and he had no idea where Simpson was looking. The end of the world as he knew it was close to him – soon there might be a bullet through his heart.

'I will do it if you are agreed, gentlemen,' he heard Masters say.

The grey sky was featureless; for this last look on the world he might as well have been blindfolded. Masters raised his voice again.

'I will say "one, two, three, fire",' he announced, 'with

those intervals. At the last word, gentlemen, you can fire as you will. Are you ready?'

'Yes,' came Simpson's voice, almost in Hornblower's ear, it seemed.

'Yes,' said Hornblower. He could hear the strain in his own voice.

'One,' said Masters, and Hornblower felt at that moment the muzzle of Simpson's pistol against his left ribs, and he raised his own.

It was in that second that he decided he could not kill Simpson even if it were in his power, and he went on lifting his pistol, forcing himself to look to see that it was pressed against the point of Simpson's shoulder. A slight wound would suffice.

'Two,' said Masters. 'Three. Fire!'

Hornblower pulled his trigger. There was a click and a spurt of smoke from the lock of his pistol. The priming had gone off but no more – his was the unloaded weapon, and he knew what it was to die. A tenth of a second later there was a click and spurt of smoke from Simpson's pistol against his heart. Stiff and still they both stood, slow to realize what had happened.

'A miss-fire, by God!' said Danvers.

The seconds crowded round them.

'Give me those pistols!' said Masters, taking them from the weak hands that held them. 'The loaded one might be hanging fire, and we don't want it to go off now.'

'Which was the loaded one?' asked Hether, consumed with curiosity.

'That is something it is better not to know,' answered Masters, changing the two pistols rapidly from hand to hand so as to confuse everyone.

'What about a second shot?' asked Danvers, and Masters looked up straight and inflexibly at him.

'There will be no second shot,' he said. 'Honour is completely satisfied. These two gentlemen have come through this ordeal extremely well. No one can now think little of Mr Simpson if he expresses his regret for the occurrence, and no one can think little of Mr Hornblower if he accepts that statement in reparation.'

Hepplewhite burst into a roar of laughter.

'Your faces!' he boomed, slapping his thigh. 'You ought to see how you all look! Solemn as cows!'

'Mr Hepplewhite,' said Masters, 'your behaviour is indecorous. Gentlemen, our coaches are waiting on the road, the cutter is at the jetty. And I think all of us would be the better for some breakfast; including Mr Hepplewhite.'

That should have been the end of the incident. The excited talk which had gone round the anchored squadron about the unusual duel died away in time, although everyone knew Hornblower's name now, and not as the midshipman who was seasick in Spithead but as the man who was willing to take an even chance in cold blood. But in the *Justinian* herself there was other talk; whispers which were circulated forward and aft.

'Mr Hornblower has requested permission to speak to you, sir,' said Mr Clay, the first lieutenant, one morning while making his report to the captain.

'Oh, send him in when you go out,' said Keene, and sighed.

Ten minutes later a knock on his cabin door ushered in a very angry young man.

'Sir?' began Hornblower.

'I can guess what you're going to say,' said Keene.

'Those pistols in the duel I fought with Simpson were not loaded!'

'Hepplewhite blabbed, I suppose,' said Keene.

'And it was by your orders, I understand, sir.'

'You are quite correct. I gave those orders to Mr Masters.'

'It was an unwarrantable liberty, sir!'

That was what Hornblower meant to say, but he stumbled without dignity over the polysyllables.

'Possibly it was,' said Keene patiently, rearranging, as always, the papers on his desk.

The calmness of the admission disconcerted Hornblower, who could only splutter for the next few moments.

'I saved a life for the King's service,' went on Keene, when the spluttering died away. 'A young life. No one has suffered any harm. On the other hand, both you and Simpson have had your courage amply proved. You both know you can stand fire now, and so does everyone else.'

'You have touched my personal honour, sir,' said Hornblower, bringing out one of his rehearsed speeches, 'for that there can only be one remedy.'

'Restrain yourself, please, Mr Hornblower.' Keene shifted himself in his chair with a wince of pain as he prepared to make a speech. 'I must remind you of one salutary regulation of the Navy, to the effect that no junior officer can challenge his superior to a duel. The reasons for it are obvious – otherwise promotion would be too easy. The mere issuing of a challenge by a junior to a senior is a court-martial offence, Mr Hornblower.'

'Oh!' said Hornblower feebly.

'Now here is some gratuitous advice,' went on Keene. 'You have fought one duel and emerged with honour. That is good. Never fight another – that is better. Some people, oddly enough, acquire a taste for duelling, as a tiger acquires a taste for blood. They are never good officers, and never popular ones either.'

It was then that Hornblower realized that a great part of

the keen excitement with which he had entered the captain's cabin was due to anticipation of the giving of the challenge. There could be a morbid desire for danger—and a morbid desire to occupy momentarily the centre of the stage. Keene was waiting for him to speak, and it was hard to say anything.

'I understand, sir,' he said at last.

Keene shifted in his chair again.

'There is another matter I wanted to take up with you, Mr Hornblower. Captain Pellew of the *Indefatigable* has room for another midshipman. Captain Pellew is partial to a game of whist, and has no good fourth on board. He and I have agreed to consider favourably your application for a transfer should you care to make one. I don't have to point out that any ambitious young officer would jump at the chance of serving in a frigate.'

'A frigate!' said Hornblower.

Everybody knew of Pellew's reputation and success. Distinction, promotion, prize money – an officer under Pellew's command could hope for all these. Competition for nomination to the *Indefatigable* must be intense, and this was the chance of a lifetime. Hornblower was on the point of making a glad acceptance, when further considerations restrained him.

'That is very good of you, sir,' he said. 'I do not know how to thank you. But you accepted me as a midshipman here, and of course I must stay with you.'

The drawn, apprehensive face relaxed into a smile.

'Not many men would have said that,' said Keene. 'But I am going to insist on your accepting the offer. I shall not live very much longer to appreciate your loyalty. And this ship is not the place for you – this ship with her useless captain – don't interrupt me – and her worn-out first lieutenant and her old midshipmen. You should be

35

where there may be speedy opportunities of advancement. I have the good of the service in mind, Mr Hornblower, when I suggest you accept Captain Pellew's invitation – and it might be less disturbing for me if you did.'

'Aye aye, sir,' said Hornblower.

The Cargo of Rice

THE wolf was in among the sheep. The tossing grey water of the Bay of Biscay was dotted with white sails as far as the eye could see, and although a strong breeze was blowing every vessel was under perilously heavy canvas. Every ship but one was trying to escape; the exception was His Majesty's frigate *Indefatigable*, Captain Sir Edward Pellew. She had come surging up from leeward upon an unescorted convoy of French merchant vessels, cutting off all chance of escape in that direction. Ship after ship was overhauled; a shot or two, and the newfangled tricolour came fluttering down from the gaff, and a prize-crew was hurriedly sent on board to conduct the captive to an English port while the frigate dashed after fresh prey.

On the quarter-deck of the *Indefatigable* Pellew fumed over each necessary delay. The brig they were pursuing at the moment was slow to surrender. The long nine-pounders in the *Indefatigable*'s bows bellowed out more than once; on that heaving sea it was not so easy to aim accurately and the brig continued on her course hoping for some miracle to save her.

'Very well,' snapped Pellew. 'He has asked for it. Let him have it.'

The gunlayers at the bow chasers changed their point of aim, firing at the ship instead of across her bows.

'Not into the hull, damn it,' shouted Pellew – one shot had struck the brig perilously close to her waterline. 'Cripple her.'

The next shot by luck or by judgement was given better

37

elevation. The slings of the foretopsail yard were shot away, the reefed sail came down, the yard hanging lop-sidedly, and the brig came up into the wind for the *Indefatigable* to heave to close beside her, her broadside ready to fire into her. Under that threat her flag came down.

'What brig's that?' shouted Pellew through his mega-phone.

'*Marie Galante* of Bordeaux,' translated the officer beside Pellew as the French captain made reply. 'Twenty-four days out from New Orleans with rice.'

'Rice!' said Pellew. 'That'll sell for a pretty penny when we get her home. Two hundred tons, I should say. Twelve of a crew at most. She'll need a prize-crew of four, a midshipman's command.'

He looked round him as though for inspiration before giving his next order.

'Mr Hornblower!'

'Sir!'

'Take four men of the cutter's crew and board that brig. Mr Soames will give you our position. Take her into any English port you can make, and report there for orders.'

'Aye aye, sir.'

Hornblower was at his station at the starboard quarter-deck carronades, his dirk at his side and a pistol in his belt. It was a moment for fast thinking, for anyone could see Pellew's impatience. With the *Indefatigable* cleared for action, his sea chest would be part of the surgeon's operating table down below, so that there was no chance of getting anything out of it. He would have to leave just as he was. The cutter was even now clawing up to a position on the *Indefatigable*'s quarter, so he ran to the ship's side and hailed her, trying to make his voice sound as big and as manly as he could, and at the word of the lieutenant in command she turned her bows in towards the frigate.

'Here's our latitude and longitude, Mr Hornblower,' said Soames, the master, handing a scrap of paper to him.

'Thank you,' said Hornblower, shoving it into his pocket.

He scrambled awkwardly into the mizen-chains and looked down into the cutter. Ship and boat were pitching together, almost bows on to the sea, and the distance between them looked appallingly great. Hornblower hesitated for a long second, but he had to make the leap, for Pellew was fuming behind him and the eyes of the boat's crew and of the whole ship's company were on him. Better to jump and hurt himself, better to jump and make an exhibition of himself, than to delay the ship. Hornblower braced himself and leaped. His feet reached the gunwale and he tottered there for one indescribable second. A seaman grabbed the breast of his jacket and he fell forward rather than backward. Not even the stout arm of the seaman, fully extended, could hold him up, and he pitched headforemost, legs in the air, upon the hands on the second thwart. He cannoned on to their bodies, knocking the breath out of his own against their muscular shoulders, and finally struggled into an upright position.

'I'm sorry,' he gasped to the men who had broken his fall.

'Never you mind, sir,' said the nearest one, a real tarry sailor, tattooed and pigtailed. 'You're only a featherweight.'

The lieutenant in command was looking at him from the sternsheets.

'Would you go to the brig, please, sir?' he asked, and

the lieutenant bawled an order and the cutter swung round as Hornblower made his way aft.

'Are you taking charge of the brig?' asked the lieutenant.

'Yes, sir. The captain told me to take four of your men.'

'They had better be topmen, then,' said the lieutenant, casting his eyes aloft at the rigging of the brig. The fore-topsail yard was hanging precariously, and the jib halliard had slacked off so that the sail was flapping thunderously in the wind. He shouted four names, and four men replied.

'Keep 'em away from drink and they'll be all right,' said the lieutenant. 'Watch the French crew. They'll recapture the ship and have you in a French gaol before you can say "Jack Robinson", if you don't.'

The cutter surged alongside the brig, white water creaming between the two vessels. The tattooed sailor sprang for the main-chains. Another man followed him, and they stood and waited while Hornblower hurled himself, all arms and legs, like a leaping frog, after them. His hands reached the shrouds, but his knee slipped off, and the brig, rolling, lowered him thigh deep into the sea as the shrouds slipped through his hands. But the waiting seamen grabbed his wrists and hauled him on board, and two more seamen followed him. He led the way on to the deck.

The first sight to meet his eyes was a man seated on the hatch cover, his head thrown back, holding to his mouth a bottle, the bottom pointing straight up to the sky. He was one of a large group all sitting round the hatch cover; a case still a quarter full of bottles stood on the deck near by. One of the seamen picked out a bottle to look at it curiously. Hornblower did not need to remember the

Hornblower braced himself and leaped

lieutenant's warning; on his shore excursions with press gangs he had already had experience of the British seaman's tendency to drink. His boarding party would be as drunk as the Frenchmen in half an hour if he allowed it.

'Put that down,' he ordered.

The urgency of the situation made his seventeen-year-old voice crack like a fourteen-year-old's, and the seaman hesitated, holding the bottle in his hand.

'Put it down, d'ye hear?' said Hornblower, desperate with worry. This was his first independent command; conditions were absolutely novel, and excitement brought out all the passion of his mercurial temperament, while at the same time the more calculating part of his mind told him that if he were not obeyed now he never would be. His pistol was in his belt, and he put his hand on the butt, and it is conceivable that he would have drawn it and used it, but the seaman, with one more glance at him, put the bottle back into the case. The incident was closed, and it was time for the next step.

'Take these men forrard,' he said, giving the obvious order. 'Throw 'em into the forecastle.'

'Aye aye, sir.'

Most of the Frenchmen could still walk, but three were dragged by their collars, while the British herded the others before them. Hornblower dragged the case of bottles down to the ship's side and pitched them overboard two at a time.

The task was finished before the last of the Frenchmen disappeared into the forecastle, and Hornblower had time to look about him. The strong breeze blew confusingly round his ears, and the ceaseless thunder of the flapping jib made it hard to think as he looked at the ruin aloft. The ship must be properly hove to, and Hornblower could guess how to set about it, and he formulated the order in his mind just in time to avoid any appearance of hesitation.

'Brace the after yards to larboard,' he said. 'Man the braces, men.'

The seaman took his competence gratifyingly for granted, but Hornblower, looking at the tangle on the foremast, had not the remotest idea of how to deal with the next problem. He was not even sure about what was wrong. But the hands under his orders were seamen of vast experience, who must have dealt with similar emergencies a score of times. The first – indeed the only – thing to do was to delegate his responsibility.

'Who's the oldest seaman among you?' he demanded – his determination not to quaver made him curt.

'Matthews, sir,' said someone at length, indicating with his thumb the pigtailed and tattoed seaman upon whom he had fallen in the cutter.

'Very well, then. I'll rate you petty officer, Matthews. Get to work at once and clear that raffle away forrard. I'll be busy here aft.'

It was a nervous moment for Hornblower, but Matthews put his knuckles to his forehead.

'Aye aye, sir,' he said, quite as a matter of course.

'Get that jib in first, before it flogs itself to pieces,' said Hornblower, greatly emboldened.

'Aye aye, sir.'

'Carry on, then.'

The seaman turned to go forward, and Hornblower walked aft. He took the telescope from its becket on the poop, and swept the horizon. Far away to windward he could see the *Indefatigable*'s topsails as she clawed after the rest of the convoy. Soon he would be alone on this wide sea, three hundred miles from England. Three hundred miles – two days with a fair wind; but how long if the wind turned foul?

As he replaced the telescope, Matthews hurried aft and knuckled his forehead.

'Beg pardon, sir, but we'll have to use the jeers to sling that yard again.'

'Very good.'

'We'll need more hands than we have, sir. Can I put some o' they Frenchies to work?'

'If you think you can. If any of them are sober enough.'

'I think I can, sir. Drunk or sober.'

'Very good.'

While Matthews went forward Hornblower went below to look around. There was a case of pistols in the captain's cabin, with a powder flask and bullet bag hanging beside it. He loaded both weapons and reprimed his own, and came on deck again with three pistols in his belt just as his men appeared from the forecastle herding half a dozen Frenchmen. He posed himself in the poop, straddling with his hands behind his back, trying to adopt an air of magnificent indifference and understanding. With the jeers taking the weight of yard and sail, an hour's hard work resulted in the yard being slung again and the sail reset.

When the work was advancing towards completion, Hornblower came to himself again to remember that in a few minutes he would have to set a course, and he dashed below again to set out the chart and the dividers and parallel rulers. From his pocket he extracted the crumpled scrap of paper with his position on it, bent over the chart, plotted his position, and laid off his course. It was a queer, uncomfortable feeling to think that what had up to this moment been an academic exercise conducted under the reassuring supervision of Mr Soames was now something on which hinged his life and his reputation. He checked his working, decided on his course, and wrote it down on a scrap of paper for fear he should forget it. So when the foretopsail yard was re-slung, and the prisoners herded back into the forecastle, and Matthews looked to him for further orders, he was ready.

'We'll square away,' he said. 'Matthews, send a man to the wheel.'

He himself gave a hand at the braces; the wind had moderated and he felt his men could handle the brig under her present sail.

'What course, sir?' asked the man at the wheel, and Hornblower dived into his pocket for his scrap of paper.

'Nor'-east by north,' he said, reading it out.

'Nor'-east by north, sir,' said the helmsman; and the *Marie Galante*, running free, set her course for England.

Night was closing in by now; there was so much to do, so much to bear in mind, and all the responsibility lay on his unaccustomed shoulders. The prisoners had to be battened down in the forecastle, a watch had to be set – a hand forward as a look-out, who could also keep an eye on the prisoners below; a hand aft at the wheel. Two hands snatching some sleep – knowing that to get in any sail would be an all-hands job – a hasty meal of water from the scuttle-butt and of biscuit from the cabin stores in the lazarette – a constant eye to be kept on the weather. Hornblower paced the deck in the darkness.

'Why don't you get some sleep, sir?' asked the man at the wheel.

'I will, later on, Hunter,' said Hornblower, trying not to allow his tone to reveal the fact that such a thing had never occurred to him.

He knew it was sensible advice, and he actually tried to follow it, retiring below to fling himself down on the captain's cot; but of course he could not sleep. When he heard the look-out bawling down the companion-way to rouse the other two hands to relieve the watch (they were asleep in the next cabin to him) he could not prevent himself from getting up again and coming on deck to see that all was well. With Matthews in charge he felt he should not be anxious, and he drove himself below again, but he had hardly fallen on to the cot again when a new thought brought him to his feet again, his skin cold with anxiety. He rushed on deck and walked forward to where Matthews was squatting by the knightheads.

'Nothing has been done to see if the brig is taking in any water,' he said. 'We'd better sound the well now.'

'Aye aye, sir,' said Matthews, without hesitation, and strolled aft to the pump. 'Not a drop, sir!' he reported on his return. 'Dry as yesterday's pannikin.'

Hornblower was agreeably surprised. Any ship he had ever heard of leaked to a certain extent; even in the well-found *Indefatigable* pumping had been necessary every day. He did not know whether this dryness was a remarkable phenomenon or a very remarkable one. He wanted to be both non-committal and imperturbable.

'H'm,' was the comment he eventually produced. The knowledge that the *Marie Galante* was making no water at all might have encouraged him to sleep, if the wind had not chosen to veer steadily and strengthen itself somewhat soon after he retired again. It was Matthews who came down and pounded on his door with the unwelcome news.

'We can't keep the course you set much longer, sir,' concluded Matthews. 'And the wind's coming gusty-like.'

'Very good, I'll be up. Call all hands,' said Hornblower, with a testiness that might have been the result of a sudden awakening if it had not really disguised his inner quaverings.

With such a small crew he dared not run the slightest risk of being taken by surprise by the weather. Nothing could be done in a hurry, as he soon found. He had to take the wheel while his four hands laboured at reefing topsails and snugging the brig down; the task took half the night, and by the time it was finished it was quite plain that with the wind veering northerly the *Marie Galante* could not steer north-east by north any longer. Hornblower gave up the wheel and went below to the chart, but what he saw there only confirmed the pessimistic decision he had already reached by mental calculation. As close to the wind as they could lie on this tack they could not weather Ushant. Short-handed as he was he did not dare continue in the hope that the wind might back; all his reading and all his instruction had warned him of the terrors of a lee shore. There was nothing for it but to go about; he returned to the deck with a heavy heart.

'All hands wear ship,' he said, trying to bellow the order in the manner of Mr Bolton, the third lieutenant of the *Indefatigable*.

They brought the brig safely round, and she took up her new course, close hauled on the starboard tack. Now she was heading away from the dangerous shores of France, without a doubt, but she was heading nearly as directly away from the friendly shores of England – gone was all hope of an easy two days' run to England; gone was any hope of sleep that night for Hornblower.

During the year before he joined the Navy Hornblower had attended classes in French. A good deal of what he had been taught had found a permanent resting-place in his tenacious memory. He had never thought it would be of much use to him, but he discovered the contrary when the French captain at dawn insisted on an interview. The Frenchman had a little English, but it was a pleasant surprise to Hornblower to find that they actually could get along better in French, as soon as he could fight down his shyness sufficiently to produce the halting words.

The captain seemed to be feeling the motion of the brig under his feet with attention.

'She rides a little heavily, does she not?' he said.

'Perhaps,' said Hornblower. He was not familiar with the *Marie Galante*, nor with ships at all, and he had no opinion on the subject, but he was not going to reveal his ignorance.

'Does she leak?' asked the captain.

'There is no water in her,' said Hornblower.

'Ah!' said the captain. 'But you would find none in the well. We are carrying a cargo of rice, you must remember.'

'Yes,' said Hornblower.

He found it very hard at that moment to remain outwardly unperturbed, as his mind grasped the implications of what was being said to him. Rice would absorb every drop of water taken in by the ship, so that no leak would be apparent on sounding the well – and yet every drop of water taken in would deprive her of that much buoyancy, all the same.

'One shot from your cursed frigate struck us in the hull,' said the captain. 'Of course you have investigated the damage?'

'Of course,' said Hornblower, lying bravely.

But as soon as he could he had a private conversation with Matthews on the point, and Matthews instantly looked grave.

'Where did the shot hit her, sir?' he asked.

'Somewhere on the port side, forrard, I should judge.'

He and Matthews craned their necks over the ship's side.

'Can't see nothin', sir,' said Matthews. 'Lower me over the side in a bowline and I'll see what I can find, sir.'

Hornblower was about to agree and then changed his mind.

'I'll go over the side myself,' he said.

Matthews and Carson put a bowline round him and lowered him over. He found himself dangling against the ship's side, with the sea bubbling just below him; as the ship pitched the sea came up to meet him, and he was wet to the waist in the first five seconds; and as the ship rolled he was alternately swung away from the side and bumped against it. The men with the line walked steadily aft, giving him the chance to examine the whole side of the brig above water, and there was not a shot-hole to be seen. He said as much to Matthews when they hauled him on deck.

'Then it's below the waterline, sir,' said Matthews, saying just what was in Hornblower's mind. 'You're sure the shot hit her, sir?'

'Yes, I'm sure,' snapped Hornblower.

Lack of sleep and worry were shortening his temper, and he had to speak sharply or break down in tears. But he had already decided on the next move.

'We'll heave her to on the other tack and try again,' he said.

On the other tack the ship would incline over to the other side, and the shot-hole, if there was one, would not be so deeply submerged. The heeling of the brig laid him much more definitely against the side, and they lowered him until his legs were scraping over the marine growths which she carried there between wind and water. They then walked aft with him, dragging him along the side of the ship, and just abaft the foremast he found what he was seeking.

'Avast, there!' he yelled up to the deck, mastering the sick despair that he felt. The motion of the bowling along the ship ceased. 'Lower away! Another two feet!'

Now he was waist-deep in the water, and when the brig swayed the water closed briefly over his head, like a momentary death. Here it was, two feet below the waterline even with the brig hove-to on this tack – a splintered, jagged hole, square rather than round, and a foot across. As the sea boiled round him Hornblower even fancied he could hear it bubbling into the ship, but that might be pure fancy.

He hailed the deck for them to haul him up again, and they stood eagerly listening for what he had to say.

'Two feet below the waterline, sir?' said Matthews. 'She was close hauled and heeling right over, of course, when we hit her. But her bows must have lifted just as we fired. And of course she's lower in the water now.'

That was the point. Whatever they did now, however much they heeled her, that hole would be under water. Something must be done to plug the leak, and Hornblower's reading of the manuals of seamanship told him what it was.

'We must fother a sail and get it over that hole,' he announced. 'Call those Frenchmen over.'

To fother a sail was to make something like a vast hairy doormat out of it, by threading innumerable lengths of half-unravelled line through it. When this was done the sail would be lowered below the ship's bottom and placed against the hole. The inward pressure would then force the hairy mass so tightly against the hole that the entrance of water would be made at least much more difficult.

The Frenchmen were not quick to help in the task; it was no longer their ship, and they were heading for an English prison, so that even with their lives at stake they were somewhat apathetic. It took time to get out a new topgallant sail and to set a party to work cutting lengths of line, threading them through, and unravelling them.

Down below, where he went in search of dry clothing, it seemed to Hornblower as if the noises all about him – the creaks and groans of a wooden ship at sea – were more pronounced than usual. The brig was riding easily enough hove-to, and yet the bulkheads were cracking and creaking as if the brig were racking herself to pieces in a storm. He dismissed the notion as a product of his over-stimulated imagination, but by the time he had towelled himself into something like warmth and put on the captain's best suit it recurred to him; the brig was groaning as if in stress.

He came on deck again to see how the working party was progressing. He had hardly been on deck two minutes when one of the Frenchmen, reaching back for another length of line, stopped in his movement to stare at the deck. He picked at a deck seam, looked up and caught Hornblower's eye, and called to him. Hornblower made no pretence of understanding the words; the gestures explained themselves. The deck seam was opening a little; the pitch was bulging out of it. Hornblower looked at the phenomenon without understanding it – only a foot or two of the seam was open, and the rest of the deck seemed solid enough. No! Now that his attention was called to it, and he looked farther, there were one or two other places in the deck where the pitch had risen in ridges from out of the seams. It was something beyond his limited experience, even beyond his extensive reading.

But the French captain was at his side staring at the deck, too.

'The cargo!' he said. 'It – it grows bigger.'

Matthews was with them now, and without knowing a word of French he understood.

'Didn't I hear this brig was full of rice, sir?' he asked.

'Yes.'

'That's it, then. The water's got into it and it's swelling.'

So it would. Dry rice soaked in water would double or treble its volume. The cargo was swelling and bursting the seams of the ship open. Hornblower remembered the unnatural creaks and groans below. It was a black moment; he looked round at the unfriendly sea for inspiration and support, and found neither. Several seconds passed before he was ready to speak, and ready to maintain the dignity of a naval officer in face of difficulties.

'The sooner we get that sail over that hole the better, then,' he said. It was too much to be expected that his voice should sound quite natural. 'Hurry those Frenchmen up.'

Even as he spoke he felt a sudden sharp shock beneath his feet, as if someone had hit the deck underneath them with a mallet. The ship was springing apart bit by bit.

'Hurry with that sail!' he yelled, turning back to the working party, and then was angry with himself because the tone of his voice must have betrayed undignified agitation.

At last an area five feet square of the sail was fothered, lines were rove through the grommets, and the working party hurried forward to work the sail under the brig and drag it aft to the hole. Hornblower was taking off his clothes, not out of regard for the captain's property but so as to keep them dry for himself.

'I'll go over and see that it's in place,' he said. 'Matthews, get a bowline ready for me.'

Naked and wet, it seemed to him as if the wind blew clear through him; rubbing against the ship's side as she rolled he lost a good deal of skin, and the waves passing down the ship smacked at him with a boisterous lack of consideration. But he saw the fothered sail placed against the hole, and with intense satisfaction he saw the hairy mass suck into position, dimpling over the hole to form a deep hollow so that he could be sure that the hole was plugged solid. They hauled him up again when he hailed, and awaited his orders; he stood naked, stupid with cold and fatigue and lack of sleep, struggling to form his next decision.

'Lay her on the starboard tack,' he said at length.

When he had dressed again he found Matthews was awaiting him with a long face.

'Sir,' he said, 'begging your pardon, but I don't like the looks of it. Straight, I don't. I don't like the feel of her. She's settlin' down and she's openin' up, I'm certain sure. Beg your pardon, sir, for saying so.'

Down below Hornblower had heard the fabric of the ship continuing to crack and complain; up here the deck seams were gaping more widely. The swelling of the rice must have forced open the ship's seams and water must still be pouring in, the cargo still swelling, opening up the ship like an overblown flower.

'Look'e there, sir!' said Matthews suddenly.

In the broad light of day a small grey shape was hurrying along the weather scuppers; another one followed it and another after that. Rats! Something convulsive must be going on down below to bring them on deck in daytime. Hornblower felt another small shock beneath his feet at that moment, as something further parted beneath them. But there was one more card to play, one last line of defence that he could think of.

'I'll jettison the cargo,' said Hornblower. He had never uttered that word in his life, but he had read it. 'Get the prisoners and we'll start.'

The battened-down hatch cover was domed upwards curiously and significantly; as the wedges were knocked out one plank tore loose at one end with a crash, pointing diagonally upwards, and as the working party lifted off the cover a brown form followed it upwards – a bag of rice, forced out by the underlying pressure until it jammed in the hatchway.

'Tail on to those tackles and sway it up,' said Hornblower.

Bag by bag the rice was hauled up from the hold; sometimes the bags split, allowing a torrent of rice to pour on to the deck, but that did not matter. Another section of the working party swept rice and bags to the lee side and into the ever-hungry sea. After the first three bags the difficulties increased, for the cargo was so tightly jammed below that it called for enormous force to tear each bag out of its position. Two men had to go down the hatchway to pry the bags loose and adjust the slings. The labour was enormous as it went on hour after hour; the men at the tackles were dripping with sweat and drooping with fatigue, but they had to relieve periodically the men below, for the bags had jammed themselves in tiers, pressed hard against the ship's bottom below and the deck beams above, and when the bags immediately below the hatchway had been swayed up the surrounding ones had to be pried loose, out of each tier. Then when a small clearance had been made in the neighbourhood of the hatchway, and they were getting deeper down into the hold, they made the inevitable discovery. The lower tiers of bags had been wetted, their contents had swelled, and the bags had burst. The lower half of the hold was packed solid with damp rice which could only be got out with shovels and a hoist.

Hornblower, facing the problems, was distracted by a touch on his elbow when Matthews came up to speak to him.

'It ain't no go, sir,' said Matthews. 'She's lower in the water an' settlin' fast.'

Hornblower walked to the ship's side with him and looked over. There could be no doubt about it. He had been over the side himself and could remember the height of the waterline, and he had for a more exact guide the level of the fothered sail under the ship's bottom. The brig was a full six inches lower in the water – and this after fifty tons of rice at least had been hoisted out and flung over the side. The brig must be leaking like a basket, with water pouring in through the gaping seams to be sucked up immediately by the thirsty rice.

Hornblower's left hand was hurting him, and he looked down to discover that he was gripping the rail with it so tightly as to cause him pain, without knowing he was doing so. He released his grip and looked about him, at the afternoon sun, at the tossing sea. He did not want to give in and admit defeat. The French captain came up to him.

'This is folly,' he said. 'Madness, sir. My men are overcome by fatigue.'

Over by the hatchway, Hornblower saw, Hunter was driving the French seamen to their work with a rope's end, which he was using furiously. There was not much more work to be got out of the Frenchmen; and at that moment the *Marie Galante* rose heavily to a wave and wallowed down the farther side. Even his inexperience could detect the sluggishness and ominous deadness of her movements. The brig had not much longer to float, and there was a good deal to do.

'I shall make preparations for abandoning the ship, Matthews,' he said.

He poked his chin upwards as he spoke; he would not allow either a Frenchman or a seaman to guess at his despair.

'Aye aye, sir,' said Matthews.

The *Marie Galante* carried a boat on chocks abaft the mainmast; at Matthews' summons the men abandoned their work on the cargo and hurried to the business of putting food and water in her. The tackles were manned and the boat was swayed up from the chocks and lowered into the water in the tiny lee afforded on the lee quarter. The *Marie Galante* put her nose into a wave, refusing to rise to it; green water came over the starboard bow and poured aft along the deck before a sullen wallow on the part of the brig sent it into the scuppers. There was not much time to spare – a rending crash from below told that the cargo was still swelling and forcing the bulkheads. There was a panic among the Frenchmen, who began to tumble down into the boat with loud cries. The French captain took one look at Hornblower and then followed them; two of the British seamen were already over the side fending off the boat.

'Go along,' said Hornblower to Matthews and Carson, who still lingered. He was the captain; it was his place to leave the ship last.

So waterlogged was the brig now that it was not at all difficult to step down into the boat from the deck; the British seamen were in the sternsheets and made room for him.

'Take the tiller, Matthews,' said Hornblower; he did

not feel he was competent to handle that over-loaded boat. 'Shove off, there!'

The boat and the brig parted company; the *Marie Galante*, with her helm lashed, poked her nose into the wind and hung there. She had acquired a sudden list, with the starboard side scuppers nearly under water. Another wave broke over her deck, pouring up to the open hatchway. Now she righted herself, her deck nearly level with the sea, and then she sank, on an even keel, the water closing over her, her masts slowly disappearing. For an instant her sails even gleamed under the green water.

'She's gone,' said Matthews.

Hornblower watched the disappearance of his first command. The *Marie Galante* had been entrusted to him to bring into port, and he had failed, failed on his first independent mission. He looked very hard at the setting sun, hoping no one would notice the tears that were filling his eyes.

A Cutting-out Expedition

Hornblower and his men succeeded in regaining the Indefatigable *after the loss of the* Marie Galante *by an unexpected reversal of fortune. After three days in the open
boat they were picked up by the* Pique, *a French privateer,
and taken prisoners. The* Pique *continued her cruise in
search of English merchantmen, but encountered the* Indefatigable *instead and turned to fly before the more powerful
but slower British ship. She was outdistancing her pursuer
with ease when Hornblower, desperate at the thought of
losing this chance of regaining his liberty, contrived to set her
on fire. With sails and rigging ablaze the privateer was
quickly overhauled and captured. Hornblower's action not
only saved him from spending the next eight years till peace
was restored rotting in a French prison, but also led to the
taking of a valuable prize, for the fire in the* Pique *was
eventually put out and she was sailed back to England in
spite of the damage it had done. The* Indefatigable *returned to her business of seeking out and destroying any
French shipping that dared to venture out of harbour.*

THIS time the wolf was prowling round outside the
sheepfold. H.M. frigate *Indefatigable* had chased the
French corvette *Papillon* into the mouth of the
Gironde, and was seeking a way of attacking her where
she lay at anchor in the stream under the protection of the
batteries at the mouth. Captain Pellew took his ship into
shoal water as far as he dared, until in fact the batteries

fired warning shots to make him keep his distance, and he stared long and keenly through his glass at the corvette. Then he shut his telescope and turned on his heel to give the order that worked the *Indefatigable* away from the dangerous lee shore – out of sight of land, in fact. His departure might lull the French into a sense of security which, he hoped, would prove unjustified. For he had no intention of leaving them undisturbed.

Midshipman Hornblower was walking the lee side of the quarter-deck, as became his lowly station as the junior officer of the watch, in the afternoon, when Midshipman Kennedy delivered an invitation to dine with the captain.

Kennedy laid one finger alongside his nose.

'Something's brewing,' he said, 'and I suppose one of these days we shall know what it is.'

There was no sign of anything brewing while dinner was being eaten in the great cabin of the *Indefatigable*. Pellew was a courtly host at the head of the table. Conversation flowed freely and along indifferent channels among the senior officers present – the two lieutenants, Eccles and Chadd, and the sailing master, Soames. Hornblower and the other junior officer – Mallory, a midshipman of over two years' seniority – kept silent, as midshipmen should, thereby being able to devote their undivided attention to the food, so vastly superior to what was served in the midshipmens' berth.

'A glass of wine with you, Mr Hornblower,' said Pellew, raising his glass.

Hornblower tried to bow gracefully in his seat while raising his glass. He sipped cautiously, for he had early found that he had a weak head, and he disliked feeling drunk.

The table was cleared and there was a brief moment of expectancy as the company awaited Pellew's next move.

'Now, Mr Soames,' said Pellew, 'let us have that chart.'

It was a map of the mouth of the Gironde, with the soundings; somebody had pencilled in the positions of the shore batteries.

'The *Papillon*,' said Sir Edward (he did not condescend to pronounce it French-fashion), 'lies just here. Mr Soames took the bearings.'

He indicated a pencilled cross on the chart, far up the channel.

'You gentlemen,' went on Pellew, 'are going in with the boats to fetch her out.'

So that was it. A cutting-out expedition.

'Mr Eccles will be in general command. I will ask him to tell you his plan.'

The grey-haired first lieutenant with the surprisingly young blue eyes looked round at the others.

'I shall have the launch,' he said, 'and Mr Soames the cutter. Mr Chadd and Mr Mallory will command the first and second gigs. And Mr Hornblower will command the jolly-boat. Each of the boats except Mr Hornblower's will have a junior officer second in command.'

That would not be necessary for the jolly-boat with its crew of seven. The launch and cutter would carry from thirty to forty men each, and the gigs twenty each; it was a large force that was being dispatched – nearly half the ship's company.

'She's a ship of war,' explained Eccles, reading their thoughts. 'No merchantman. Ten guns a side, and full of men.'

Nearer two hundred men than a hundred, certainly – plentiful opposition for a hundred and twenty British seamen.

'But we will be attacking her by night and taking her by surprise,' said Eccles, reading their thoughts again.

'Surprise,' put in Pellew, 'is more than half the battle, as you know, gentlemen – please pardon the interruption, Mr Eccles.'

'At the moment,' went on Eccles, 'we are out of sight of land. We are about to stand in again. We have never hung about this part of the coast, and the Frogs'll think we've gone for good. We'll make the land after nightfall, stand in as far as possible, and then the boats will go in. High water tomorrow morning is at four-fifty; dawn is at five-thirty. The attack will be delivered at four-thirty so that the watch below will have had time to get to sleep. The launch will attack on the starboard quarter, and the cutter on the larboard quarter. Mr Mallory's gig will attack on the larboard bow, and Mr Chadd's on the starboard bow. Mr Chadd will be responsible for cutting the corvette's cable as soon as he has mastered the forecastle, and the other boats' crews have at least reached the quarter-deck.'

Eccles looked round at the other three commanders of the large boats, and they nodded understanding. Then he went on.

'Mr Hornblower with the jolly-boat will wait until the attack has gained a foothold on the deck. He will then board at the main-chains, either to starboard or larboard as he sees fit, and he will at once ascend the main rigging, paying no attention to whatever fighting is going on on deck. He will see to it that the maintopsail is loosed and he will sheet it home on receipt of further orders. I myself, or Mr Soames in the event of my being killed or wounded, will send two hands to the wheel and will attend to steering the corvette as soon as she is under way. The tide will take us out, and the *Indefatigable* will be awaiting us just out of gunshot from the shore batteries.'

'Any comments, gentlemen?' asked Pellew.

That was the moment when Hornblower should have spoken up – the only moment when he could. Eccles' orders had set in motion sick feelings of apprehension in his stomach. Hornblower was no maintopman, and Hornblower knew it. He hated heights, and he hated going aloft. He knew he had none of the monkey-like agility and self-confidence of the good seaman. He was unsure of himself aloft in the dark even in the *Indefatigable*, and he was utterly appalled at the thought of going aloft in an entirely strange ship and finding his way among strange rigging. He felt himself quite unfitted for the duty assigned to him, and he should have raised a protest at once on account of his unfitness. But he let the opportunity pass, for he was overcome by the matter-of-fact way in which the other officers accepted the plan. He looked round at the unmoved faces; nobody was paying any attention to him, and he jibbed at making himself conspicuous. He swallowed; he even got as far as opening his mouth, but still no one looked at him, and his protest died stillborn.

'Very well, then, gentlemen,' said Pellew. 'I think you had better go into the details, Mr Eccles.'

Then it was too late. Eccles, with the chart before him,

was pointing out the course to be taken through the shoals and mudbanks of the Gironde, and expatiating on the position of the shore batteries. Hornblower listened, trying to concentrate despite his apprehensions. Eccles finished his remarks and Pellew closed the meeting.

'Since you all know your duties, gentlemen, I think you should start your preparations. The sun is about to set and you will find you have plenty to do.'

The boats' crews had to be told off; it was necessary to see that the men were armed, and that the boats were provisioned in case of emergency. Every man had to be instructed in the duties expected of him. And Hornblower had to rehearse himself in ascending the main shrouds and laying out along the maintopsail yard. Twice he made the whole journey, battling with the disquiet of his stomach at the thought of the hundred-foot drop below him. Finally, gulping with nervousness, he transferred his grip to the brace and forced himself to slide down it to the deck – that would be his best route when the time came to sheet the topsail home. He was by no means satisfied with himself even when he reached the deck, and at the back of his mind was a vivid mental picture of his missing his hold when the time came for him to repeat the performance in the *Papillon*, and falling headlong to the deck – a second or two of frightful fear while rushing through the air, and then a shattering crash. And the success of the attack hinged on him, as much as on anyone – if the topsail were not promptly set to give the corvette steerage way she would run aground on one of the innumerable shoals in the river mouth to be ignominiously recaptured, and half the crew of the *Indefatigable* would be dead or prisoners.

In the waist the jolly-boat's crew was formed up for his inspection. He saw to it that the oars were properly muffled, that each man had pistol and cutlass, and made sure that every pistol was at half-cock so that there was no fear of a premature shot giving warning of the attack. He allocated duties to each man in the loosening of the topsail, laying stress on the possibility that casualties might necessitate unrehearsed changes in the scheme.

'I will mount the rigging first,' said Hornblower.

That had to be the case. He had to lead – it was expected of him. More than that: if he had given any other order it would have excited comment – and contempt.

'Jackson,' went on Hornblower, addressing the coxswain, 'you will quit the boat last and take command if I fall.'

'Aye aye, sir.'

It was usual to use the poetic expression 'fall' for 'die', and it was only after Hornblower had uttered the word that he thought about its horrible real meaning in the present circumstances.

'Is that all understood?' asked Hornblower harshly; it was his mental stress that made his voice grate so.

Everyone nodded, and Hornblower dismissed them.

There were some hours yet to wait while the *Indefatigable* crept inshore, with the lead going steadily and Pellew himself attending to the course of the frigate. Hornblower, despite his nervousness and his miserable apprehensions, yet found time to appreciate the superb seamanship displayed as Pellew brought the big frigate in through these tricky waters on that dark night. His interest was so caught by the procedure that the little tremblings which had been assailing him ceased to manifest themselves; Hornblower was of the type that would continue to observe and to learn on his deathbed. By the time the *Indefatigable* had reached the point off the mouth of the river where it was desirable to launch the boats, Hornblower had learned a good deal about the practical application of the principles of coastwise navigation and a good deal about the organization of a cutting-out expedition – and by self-analysis he had learned even more about the psychology of a raiding party before a raid.

He had mastered himself to all outside appearance by the time he went down into the jolly-boat as she heaved on the inky-black water, and he gave the command to shove off in a quiet, steady voice. Hornblower took the tiller – the feel of that solid bar of wood was reassuring, and it was old habit now to sit in the stern sheets with hand and elbow upon it, and the men began to pull slowly after the dark shapes of the four big boats; there was plenty of time, and the flowing tide would take them up the estuary. That was just as well, for on one side of them lay the batteries of St Dye, and inside the estuary on the other side was the fortress of Blaye; forty big guns trained to sweep the channel, and none of the five boats – certainly not the jolly-boat – could withstand a single shot from one of them.

He kept his eyes attentively on the cutter ahead of him. Soames had the dreadful responsibility of taking the boats up the channel, while all he had to do was to follow in her wake – all, except to loose that maintopsail. Hornblower found himself shivering again.

Silently the boats glided up the estuary; Soames in the cutter was setting a slow pace, with only an occasional stroke at the oars to maintain steerage way. Presumably he knew very well what he was doing; the channel he had selected was an obscure one between mudbanks, impracticable for anything except small boats, and he had a twenty-foot pole with him with which to take the soundings – quicker and much more silent than using the lead. Minutes were passing fast, and yet the night was still utterly dark, with no hint of approaching dawn. Strain his eyes as he would Hornblower could not be sure that he could see the flat shores on either side of him. It would call for sharp eyes on the land to detect the little boats being carried up by the tide.

Far away ahead – in the darkness it was impossible to estimate the distance – there was a nucleus of greater darkness, close on the surface of the black water. It might be the corvette. A dozen more silent strokes, and Hornblower was sure of it. Soames had done a magnificent job of pilotage, leading the boats straight to that objective. The cutter and launch were diverging now from the two gigs. The four boats were separating in readiness to launch their simultaneous converging attack.

'Easy!' whispered Hornblower, and the jolly-boat's crew ceased to pull.

Hornblower had his orders. He had to wait until the attack had gained a foothold on the deck. Although he could see the corvette, the boats had vanished from his sight, had passed out of his field of vision. The corvette rode to her anchor, her spars just visible against the night sky – that was where he had to climb! She seemed to tower up hugely. Close by the corvette he saw a splash in the dark water – the boats were closing in fast and someone's stroke had been a little careless. At the same moment came a shout from the corvette's deck, and when the shout was repeated it was echoed a hundredfold from the boats rushing alongside. The yelling was lusty and prolonged, of set purpose. A sleeping enemy would be bewildered by the din, and the progress of the shouting would tell each boat's crew of the extent of the success of the others. The British seamen were yelling like madmen. A flash and a bang from the corvette's deck told of the firing of the first shot; soon pistols were popping and muskets banging from several points of the deck.

'Give way!' said Hornblower. He uttered the order as if it had been torn from him by the rack.

The jolly-boat moved forward, while Hornblower fought down his feelings and tried to make out what was going on on board. He could see no reason for choosing either side of the corvette in preference to the other, and the larboard side was the nearer, and so he steered the boat to the larboard main-chains. So interested was he in what he was doing that he only remembered in the nick of time to give the order, 'In oars.' He put the tiller over and the boat swirled round and the bowman hooked on. From the deck just above came a noise exactly like a tinker hammering on a cooking-pot – Hornblower noted the curious noise as he stood up in the stern sheets. He felt the cutlass at his side and the pistol in his belt, and then he sprang for the chains. With a mad leap he reached them and hauled himself up. The shrouds came into his hands, his feet found the ratlines beneath them, and he began to climb. As his head cleared the bulwark and he could see the deck the flash of a pistol-shot illuminated the scene momentarily, fixing the struggle on the deck in a static moment, like a picture. Before and below him a British seaman was fighting a furious cutlass duel with a French officer, and he realized with vague astonishment that the kettle-mending noise he had heard was the sound of cutlass against cutlass – that clash of steel against steel that poets wrote about. So much for romance.

The realization carried him far up the shrouds. At his elbow he felt the futtock shrouds and he transferred himself to them, hanging back downward with his toes hooked into the ratlines and his hands clinging like death. That only lasted for two or three desperate seconds, and then he hauled himself on to the topmast shrouds and began the final ascent, his lungs bursting with the effort. Here was the topsail yard, and Hornblower flung himself across it and felt with his feet for the foot-rope. Merciful God! There was no foot-rope – his feet searching in the darkness met only unresisting air. A hundred feet above the deck he hung, squirming and kicking like a baby held up at arm's length in its father's hands. There was no foot-rope; it may have been with this very situation in mind that the Frenchmen had removed it. There was no foot-rope, so that he could not make his way out to the yard-arm. Yet the gaskets must be cast off and the sail loosed – everything depended on that. Hornblower had seen daredevil seamen run out along the yards standing upright, as though walking a tightrope. That was the only way to reach the yard-arm now.

For a moment he could not breathe as his weak flesh revolted against the thought of walking along that yard above the black abyss. This was fear, the fear that stripped a man of his manhood, turning his bowels to water and his limbs to paper. Yet his furiously active mind continued to work. This was cowardice, the sort of thing that men spoke about behind their hands to other men. He could not bear the thought of that in himself – it was worse (awful though the alternative might be) than the thought of falling through the night to the deck. With a gasp he brought his knee up on to the yard, heaving himself up until he stood upright. He felt the rounded, canvas-covered timber under his feet, and his instincts told him not to dally there for a moment.

'Come on, men!' he yelled, and he dashed out along the yard.

It was twenty feet to the yard-arm, and he covered the distance in a few frantic strides. Utterly reckless by now, he put his hands down on the yard, clasped it, and laid his body across it again, his hands seeking the gaskets. A thump on the yard told him that Oldroyd, who had been detailed to come after him, had followed him out along the yard – he had six feet less to go. There could be no doubt that the other members of the jolly-boat's crew were on the yard, and that Clough had led the way to the starboard yard-arm. It was obvious from the rapidity with which the sail came loose. Here was the brace beside him. Without any thought of danger now, for he was delirious with excitement and triumph, he grasped it with both hands and jerked himself off the yard. His waving legs found the rope and twined about it, and he let himself slide down it.

Fool that he was! Would he never learn sense and prudence? Would he never remember that vigilance and precaution must never be relaxed? He had allowed himself to slide so fast that the rope seared his hands, and when he tried to tighten his grip so as to slow down his progress it caused him such agony that he had to relax it again and slide on down with the rope stripping the skin from his hands as though peeling off a glove. His feet reached the deck and he momentarily forgot the pain as he looked round him.

There was the faintest grey light beginning to show now, and there were no sounds of battle. It had been a well-worked surprise – a hundred men flung suddenly on the deck of the corvette had swept away the anchor watch and mastered the vessel in a single rush before the watch below could come up to offer any resistance. Chadd's stentorian voice came pealing from the forecastle.

'Cable's cut, sir!'

Then Eccles bellowed from aft.

'Mr Hornblower!'

'Sir!' yelled Hornblower.

'Man the halliards!'

A rush of men came to help – not only his own boat's crew but every man of initiative and spirit. Halliards, sheets and braces; the sail was trimmed round and was drawing full in the light southerly air, and the *Papillon* swung round to go down with the first of the ebb. Dawn was coming up fast, with a trifle of mist on the surface of the water.

Over the starboard quarter came a sullen bellowing roar, and then the misty air was torn by a series of infernal screams, supernaturally loud. The first cannon balls Hornblower ever heard were passing him by.

'Mr Chadd! Set the headsails! Loose the foretops'l. Get aloft, some of you, and set the mizen tops'l.'

From the port bow came another salvo – Blaye was firing at them from one side, St Dye from the other, now they could guess what had happened on board the *Papillon*. But the corvette was moving fast with wind and tide, and it would be no easy matter to cripple her in the half-light. It had been a very near-run thing; a few seconds' delay could have been fatal. Only one shot from the next salvo passed within hearing, and its passage was marked by a loud snap overhead.

'Mr Mallory, get that forestay spliced!'

'Aye aye, sir!'

It was light enough to look round the deck now; he could see Eccles at the break of the poop, directing the handling of the corvette, and Soames beside the wheel conning her down the channel. Two groups of red-coated marines, with bayonets fixed, stood guard over

It was twenty feet to the yard-arm, and he covered the distance in a few frantic strides

the hatchways. There were four or five men lying on the deck in curiously abandoned attitudes. Dead men; Hornblower could look at them with the callousness of youth. But there was a wounded man, too, crouched groaning over his shattered thigh – Hornblower could not look at him as disinterestedly, and he was glad, maybe only for his own sake, when at that moment a seaman asked for and received permission from Mallory to leave his duties and attend to him.

'Stand by to go about!' shouted Eccles from the poop; the corvette had reached the tip of the middle ground shoal and was about to make the turn that would carry her into the open sea.

The men came running to the braces, and Hornblower tailed on along with them. But the first contact with the harsh rope gave him such pain that he almost cried out. His hands were like raw meat, and fresh-killed at that, for blood was running from them. Now that his attention was called to them they smarted unbearably.

The headsail sheets came over, and the corvette went handily about.

'There's the old *Indy*!' shouted somebody.

The *Indefatigable* was plainly visible now, lying-to just out of shot from the shore batteries, ready to rendezvous with her prize. Somebody cheered, and the cheering was taken up by everyone, even while the last shot from St Dye, fired at extreme range, pitched sullenly into the water alongside. Hornblower had gingerly extracted his handkerchief from his pocket and was trying to wrap it round his hand.

'Can I help you with that, sir?' asked Jackson.

Jackson shook his head as he looked at the raw surface.

'You was careless, sir. You ought to 'a gone down 'and over 'and,' he said, when Hornblower explained to him how the injury had been caused. 'Very careless, you was, beggin' your pardon for saying so, sir. But you young gennelmen often is. You don't 'ave no thought for your necks, nor your 'ides, sir.'

Hornblower looked up at the maintopsail yard high above his head, and remembered how he had walked along that slender stick of timber out to the yard-arm in the dark. At the recollection of it, even here with the solid deck under his feet, he shuddered a little.

The Spanish Galleys

THE old *Indefatigable* was lying at anchor in the Bay
of Cadiz at the time when Spain made peace with
France. Hornblower happened to be midshipman of
the watch, and it was he who called the attention of
Lieutenant Chadd to the approach of the eight-oared
pinnace, with the red and yellow of Spain drooping at
the stern. Chadd's glass made out the gleam of gold on
epaulette and cocked hat, and bellowed the order for
sideboys and marine guard to give the traditional honours
to a captain in an allied service. Pellew, hurriedly warned,
was at the gangway to meet his visitor, and it was at
the gangway that the entire interview took place. The
Spaniard, making a low bow with his hat across his
stomach, offered a sealed envelope to the Englishman.

'Here, Mr Hornblower,' said Pellew, holding the letter
unopened, 'speak French to this fellow. Ask him to come
below for a glass of wine.'

But the Spaniard, with a further bow, declined the
refreshment, and, with another bow, requested that
Pellew open the letter immediately. Pellew broke the seal
and read the contents, struggling with the French which
he could read to a small extent although he could not
speak it at all. He handed it to Hornblower.

'This means the Dagoes have made peace, doesn't it?'

Hornblower struggled through twelve lines of compliments addressed by His Excellency the Duke of Belchite
(Grandee of the First Class, with eighteen other titles
ending with Captain-General of Andalusia) to the Most
Gallant Ship-Captain Sir Edward Pellew, Knight of the

Bath. The second paragraph was short and contained only a brief intimation of peace. The third paragraph was as long as the first, and repeated its phraseology almost word for word in a ponderous farewell.

'That's all, sir,' said Hornblower.

But the Spanish captain had a verbal message with which to supplement the written one.

'Please tell your captain,' he said, in his lisping Spanish-French, 'that now as a neutral power, Spain must enforce her rights. You have already been at anchor here for twenty-four hours. Six hours from now' – the Spaniard took a gold watch from his pocket and glanced at it – 'if you are within range of the batteries at Puntales there they will be given orders to fire on you.'

Hornblower could only translate the brutal message without any attempt at softening it, and Pellew listened, white with anger despite his tan.

'Tell him –' he began, and then mastered his rage. 'Damme if I'll let him see he has made me angry.'

He put his hat across his stomach and bowed in as faithful an imitation of the Spaniard's courtliness as he could manage, before he turned to Hornblower.

'Tell him I have received his message with pleasure. Tell him I much regret that circumstances are separating him from me, and that I hope I shall always enjoy his personal friendship whatever the relations between our countries. Tell him – oh, you can tell him the sort of thing I want said, can't you, Hornblower? Let's see him over the side with dignity. Sideboys! Bosun's mates! Drummers!'

Hornblower poured out compliments to the best of his ability, and at every phrase the two captains exchanged bows, the Spaniard withdrawing a pace at each bow and Pellew following him up, not to be outdone in courtesy.

The drums beat a ruffle, the marines presented arms, the pipes shrilled and twittered until the Spaniard's head had descended to the level of the main deck, when Pellew stiffened up, clapped his hat on his head, and swung round on his first lieutenant.

'Mr Eccles, I want to be under way within the hour, if you please.'

Then he stamped down below to regain his equanimity in private.

Hands were aloft loosing sail ready to sheet home, while the clank of the capstan told how other men were heaving the cable short, and Hornblower was standing on the portside gangway with Mr Wales, the carpenter, looking over at the white houses of one of the most beautiful cities in Europe.

'I've been ashore there twice,' said Wales. 'The wine's good – vino, they calls it – if you happens to like that kind o' muck. But don't you ever try that brandy, Mr Hornblower. Poison, it is, rank poison. Hello! We're going to have an escort, I see.'

Two long, sharp prows had emerged from the inner bay, and were pointing towards the *Indefatigable*. Hornblower could not restrain himself from giving a cry of surprise as he followed Wales's gaze. The vessels approaching were galleys; along each side of them the oars were lifting and falling rhythmically, catching the sunlight as they feathered. The effect, as a hundred oars swung like one, was perfectly beautiful. Hornblower remembered a line in a Latin poem which he had translated as a schoolboy, and recalled his surprise when he discovered that to a Roman the 'white wings' of a ship of war were her oars. Now the simile was plain; even a gull in flight, which Hornblower had always looked upon until now as displaying the perfection of motion, was not more beautiful than those galleys. They lay low in the water, immensely long for their beam. Neither the sails nor the lateen yards were set on the low, raking masts. The bows blazed with gilding, while the waters of the bay foamed round them as they headed into the teeth of the gentle breeze with the Spanish red and gold streaming aft from the masthead. Up – forward – down – went the oars with unchanging rhythm, the blades not varying an inch in their distance apart during the whole of the stroke. From the bows of each two long guns looked straight forward in the direction the galleys pointed.

'Twenty-four pounders,' said Wales. 'If they catch you in a calm, they'll knock you to pieces. Lie off on your quarter where you can't bring a gun to bear and rake you till you strike. An' then God help you – better a Turkish prison than a Spanish one.'

In a line-ahead that might have been drawn with a ruler and measured with a chain the galleys passed close along the port side of the *Indefatigable* and went ahead of her. As they passed the roll of the drum and the call of the pipes summoned the crew of the *Indefatigable* to attention out of compliment to the flag and the commission pendant going by, while the galleys' officers returned the salute.

'It don't seem right, somehow,' muttered Wales under his breath, 'to salute 'em like they was a frigate.'

Level with the *Indefatigable*'s bowsprit the leader backed her starboard side oars, and spun like a top, despite her length and narrow beam, across the frigate's bows. The gentle wind blew straight to the frigate from the galley, and then from her consort as the latter followed; and a foul stench came back on the air and assailed Hornblower's nostrils, and not Hornblower's alone, clearly, for it brought forth cries of disgust from all the men on deck.

'They all stink like that,' explained Wales. 'Four men to the oar an' fifty oars. Two hundred galley slaves, that is. All chained to their benches. When you goes aboard one of them as a slave you're chained to your bench, an' you're never unchained until they drop you overside. Sometimes when the hands aren't busy they'll hose out the bilge, but that doesn't happen often, bein' Dagoes an' not many of 'em.'

Hornblower, as always, sought exact information.

'How many, Mr Wales?'

'Thirty, mebbe. Enough to hand the sails if they're making a passage. Or to man the guns – they strike the yards and sails, like now, before they goes into action, Mr Hornblower,' said Wales, pontifical as usual. 'So you see how it is. With no more than thirty of a crew an' two hundred slaves they daren't let 'em loose, not ever.'

The galleys had turned again, and were now passing down the *Indefatigable*'s starboard side. The beat of the oars had slowed very noticeably, and Hornblower had ample time to observe the vessels closely, the low fore-castle and high poop with the gangway connecting them along the whole length of the galley; upon that gangway walked a man with a whip. The towers were invisible below the bulwarks, the oars being worked through holes in the sides closed, as far as Hornblower could see, with sheets of leather round the oar-looms to keep out the sea. On the poop stood two men at the tiller and a small group of officers, their gold lace flashing in the sunshine. Save for the gold lace and the twenty-four-pounder bow chasers Hornblower was looking at exactly the same sort of vessel as the ancients used to fight their battles. Polybius and Thucydides wrote about galleys almost identical with these – for that matter it was not much more than two hundred years since the galleys had fought their last great battle at Lepanto against the Turks. But those battles had been fought with hundreds of galleys a side.

'How many do they have in commission now?' asked Hornblower.

'A dozen, mebbe – not that I knows for sure, o' course. Carthagena's their usual station, beyond the Gut.'

Wales, as Hornblower understood, meant by this through the Strait of Gibraltar in the Mediterranean.

'Too frail for the Atlantic,' Hornblower commented.

It was easy to deduce the reasons for the survival of this small number – the innate conservatism of the Spaniards would account for it to a large extent. Then there was the point that condemnation to the galleys was one way of disposing of criminals. And when all was said and done a galley might still be useful in a calm – merchant ships becalmed while trying to pass the Strait of Gibraltar might be snapped up by galleys pushing out from Cadiz or Carthagena. And at the very lowest estimate there might be some employment for galleys to tow vessels in and out of harbour with the wind unfavourable.

'Mr Hornblower!' said Eccles. 'My respects to the captain, and we're ready to get under way.'

Hornblower dived below with his message.

'My compliments to Mr Eccles,' said Pellew, looking up from his desk, 'and I'll be on deck immediately.'

There was just enough of a southerly breeze to enable the *Indefatigable* to weather the point in safety. With her anchor catted she braced round her yards and began to steal seaward; in the disciplined stillness which prevailed the sound of the ripple of water under her cutwater was clearly to be heard – a musical note which told nothing, in its innocence, of the savagery and danger of the world of the sea into which she was entering. Creeping along under her topsails the *Indefatigable* made no more than three knots, and the galleys came surging past her again, oars beating their fastest rhythm, as if the galleys were boasting of their independence of the elements. Their gilt flashed in the sun as they overtook to windward, and once again their foul stench offended the nostrils of the men of the *Indefatigable*.

'I'd be obliged if they'd keep to leeward of us,' muttered Pellew, watching them through his glass. 'But I suppose that's not Spanish courtesy. Mr Cutler!'

'Sir!' said the gunner.

'You may commence the salute.'

'Aye aye, sir.'

The forward carronade on the lee side roared out the first of its compliments, and the fort of Puntales began its reply. The sound of the salute rolled round the beautiful bay; nation was speaking to nation in all courtesy.

'The next time we hear those guns they'll be shotted, I fancy,' said Pellew, gazing across at Puntales and the flag of Spain flying above it.

Indeed, the tide of war was turning against England. Nation after nation had retired from the contest against France, some worsted by arms, and some by the diplomacy of the vigorous young republic. To any thinking mind it was obvious that once the step from war to neutrality had been taken, the next step would be easy, from neutrality to war on the other side. Hornblower could foresee, close at hand, a time when all Europe would be arrayed in hostility to England, when she would be battling for her life against the rejuvenescent power of France and the malignity of the whole world.

'Set sail, please, Mr Eccles,' said Pellew.

Two hundred trained pairs of legs raced aloft; two hundred trained pairs of arms let loose the canvas, and the *Indefatigable* doubled her speed, heeling slightly to the gentle breeze. Now she was meeting the long Atlantic swell. So were the galleys; as the *Indefatigable* overtook them, Hornblower could see the leader put her nose into a long roller so that a cloud of spray broke over her forecastle. That was asking too much of such frail craft. Back went one bank of oars; forward went the other. The galleys rolled hideously for a moment in the trough of the sea before they completed their turn and headed back for the safe waters of Cadiz Bay. Someone forward in the *Indefatigable* began to boo, and the cry was instantly taken up through the ship. A storm of boos and whistles and catcalls pursued the galleys, the men momentarily quite out of hand while Pellew spluttered with rage on the quarter-deck and the petty officers strove in vain to take the names of the offenders. It was an ominous farewell to Spain.

Ominous indeed. It was not long before Captain Pellew gave the news to the ship that Spain had completed her change-over; with the treasure convoy safely in she had declared war against England; the revolutionary republic had won the alliance of the most decayed monarchy in Europe.

It was a day of glassy calm in the Straits of Gibraltar. The sea was like a silver shield, the sky like a bowl of sapphire, with the mountains of Africa on the one hand, the mountains of Spain on the other as dark serrations on the horizon. It was not a comfortable situation for the *Indefatigable*, but that was not because of the blazing sun which softened the pitch in the deck seams. There is almost always a slight current setting inwards into the Mediterranean from the Atlantic, and the prevailing winds blow in the same direction. In a calm like this it was not unusual for a ship to be carried far through the Straits, past the Rock of Gibraltar, and then to have to beat for days and even weeks to make Gibraltar Bay. So that Pellew was not unnaturally anxious about his convoy of grain ships from Oran. Gibraltar had to be revictualled – Spain had already marched an army up for the siege – and he dared not risk being carried past his destination. His orders to his reluctant convoy had been enforced by flag and gun signals, for no short-handed merchant ship relished the prospect of the labour Pellew wished to be executed. The *Indefatigable* no less than her convoy had lowered boats, and the helpless ships were now all in two. That was backbreaking, exhausting labour, the men at the oars tugging and straining, dragging the oar blades through the water, while the towlines tightened and bucked with superhuman perversity and the ships sheered freakishly from side to side. It was less than a mile an hour, that the ships made in this fashion, at the cost of the complete exhaustion of the boats' crews, but at least it postponed the time when the Gibraltar current would carry them to leeward, and similarly gave more chance for the longed-for southerly wind – two hours of a southerly wind was all they wished for - to waft them up to the Mole.

Down in the *Indefatigable*'s long-boat and cutter the men tugging at their oars were so stupefied with their toil that they did not hear the commotion in the ship. They were just tugging and straining under the pitiless sky, living through their two hours' spell of misery, but they were roused by the voice of the captain himself, hailing them from the forecastle.

'Mr Bolton! Mr Chadd! Cast off there, if you please. You'd better come and arm your men at once. Here come our friends from Cadiz.'

Back on the quarter-deck, Pellew looked through

his glass at the hazy horizon; he could make out from here by now what had first been reported from the mast-head.

'They're heading straight for us,' he said.

The two galleys were on their way from Cadiz; presumably a fast horseman from the lookout point at Tarifa had brought them the news of this golden opportunity, of the flat calm and the scattered and helpless convoy. This was the moment for galleys to justify their continued existence. They could capture and at least burn, although they could not hope to carry off the unfortunate merchant ships while the *Indefatigable* lay helpless, hardly out of cannon's range. Pellew looked round at the two merchant ships and the three brigs; one of them was within half a mile of him and might be covered by his gunfire, but the others – a mile and a half, two miles away – had no such protection.

'Pistols and cutlasses, my lads!' he said to the men pouring up from overside. 'Clap on to that stay tackle now. Smartly with that carronade, Mr Cutler!'

The *Indefatigable* had been in too many expeditions where minutes counted to waste any time over these preparations. The boats' crews seized their arms, the six-pounder carronades were lowered into the bows of the cutter and long-boat, and soon the boats, crowded with armed men and provisioned against sudden emergency, were pulling away to meet the galleys.

'What the devil d'you think you're doing, Mr Hornblower?'

Pellew had just caught sight of Hornblower in the act of swinging out of the jolly-boat which was his special charge. He wondered what his midshipman thought he could achieve against a war-galley with a twelve-foot boat and a crew of six.

'We can pull to one of the convoy and reinforce the crew, sir,' said Hornblower.

'Oh, very well then, carry on. I'll trust to your good sense, even though that's a broken reed.'

'Good on you, sir!' said Jackson ecstatically, as the jolly-boat shoved off from the frigate. 'Good on you! No one else wouldn't never have thought of that.'

Jackson, the coxswain of the jolly-boat obviously thought that Hornblower had no intention of carrying out his suggestion to reinforce the crew of one of the merchant ships.

'Those stinking Dagoes,' said stroke oar, between his teeth.

Hornblower was conscious of the presence in his crew of the same feeling of violent hostility towards the Spanish galleys as he felt within himself. He had never known this feeling of personal hatred before; when previously he had fought it had been as a servant of the King, not out of personal animosity. Yet here he was gripping the tiller under the scorching sky and leaning forward in his eagerness to be at actual grips with this enemy.

The longboat and cutter had a long start of them, and even though they were manned by crews who had already served a spell at the oars they were skimming over the water at such a speed that the jolly-boat with all the advantage of the glassy-smooth water only slowly caught up to them. Overside the sea was of the bluest, deepest blue until the oar blades churned it white. Ahead of them the vessels of the convoy lay scattered where the sudden calm had caught them, and just beyond them Hornblower caught sight of the flash of oar blades as the galleys came sweeping down on their prey. Longboat and cutter were diverging in an endeavour to cover as many vessels as possible, and the gig was still far astern. There would hardly be time to board a ship even if Hornblower should wish to. He put the tiller over to incline his course after the cutter; one of the galleys at that moment abruptly made its appearance in the gap between two of the merchant ships. Hornblower saw the cutter swing round to point her six-pounder carronade at the advancing bows.

'Pull, you men! Pull!' he shrieked, mad with excitement.

He could not imagine what was going to happen, but he wanted to be in the fray. That six-pounder popgun was grossly inaccurate at any range longer than musket shot. It would serve to hurl a mass of grape into a crowd of men, but its ball would have small effect on the strengthened bows of a war galley.

'Pull!' shrieked Hornblower again. He was nearly up to them, wide on the cutter's quarter.

The carronade boomed out. Hornblower thought he saw the splinters fly from the galley's bow, but the shot had no more effect on deterring her than a peashooter could stop a charging bull. The galley turned a little, getting exactly into line, and then her oars' beat quickened. She was coming down to ram, like the Greeks at Salamis.

'Pull!' shrieked Hornblower.

Instinctively, he gave the tiller a touch to take the jolly-boat out into a flanking position.

'Easy!'

The jolly-boat's oars stilled, as their way carried them past the cutter. Hornblower could see Soames standing up in the sternsheets looking at the death which was cleaving the blue water towards him. Bow to bow the cutter might have stood a chance, but too late the cutter tried to evade the blow altogether. Hornblower saw her turn, presenting her vulnerable side to the galley's stem. That was all he could see, for the next moment the galley herself hid from him the final act of the tragedy. The jolly-boat's starboard side oars only just cleared the galley's starboard oars as she swept by. Hornblower heard a shriek and a crash, saw the galley's forward motion almost cease at the collision. He was mad with the lust of fighting, quite insane, and his mind was working with the rapidity of insanity.

'Give way, port!' he yelled, and the jolly-boat swung round under the galley's stern. 'Give way all!'

The jolly-boat leaped after the galley like a terrier after a bull.

'Grapple them, damn you, Jackson!'

Jackson shouted an oath in reply, as he leaped forward, seemingly hurdling the men at the oars without breaking their stroke. In the bows Jackson seized the boat's grapnel on its long line and flung it hard and true. It caught somewhere in the elaborate gilt rail on the galley's quarter. Jackson hauled on the line, the oars tugged madly in the effort to carry the jolly-boat up to the galley's stern as the galley leaped forward again.

'I can't hold her!' shouted Jackson.

'Take a turn round the cleat, you fool!'

The galley was towing the jolly-boat now, dragging her along at the end of a twenty-foot line close on her quarter, just clear of the arc of her rudder. The white water bubbled all around her, her bows were cocked up with the strain. It was a mad moment, as though they had harpooned a whale. Someone came running aft on the Spaniard's poop, knife in hand to cut the line.

'Shoot him, Jackson!' shrieked Hornblower again.

Jackson's pistol cracked, and the Spaniard fell to the deck out of sight – a good shot. Despite his fighting madness, despite the turmoil of rushing water and glaring sun, Hornblower tried to think out his next move. Inclination and common sense alike told him that the best plan was to close with the enemy despite the odds.

'Pull up to them, there!' he shouted – everyone in the boat was shouting and yelling. The men in the bows of the jolly-boat faced forward and took the grapnel line and began to haul in on it, but the speed of the boat through the water made any progress difficult, and after a yard or so had been gained the difficulty became insurmountable, for the grapnel was caught in the poop rail ten or eleven feet above water, and the angle of pull became progressively steeper as the jolly-boat neared the stern of the galley. The boat's bow cocked higher out of the water than ever.

'Belay!' said Hornblower, and then, his voice rising again, 'Out pistols, lads!'

A row of four or five swarthy faces had appeared at the stern of the galley. Muskets were pointing into the jolly-boat, and there was a brief but furious exchange of shots. One man fell groaning into the bottom of the jolly-boat, but the row of faces disappeared. Standing up precariously in the swaying sternsheets, Hornblower could still see nothing of the galley's poop deck save for the tops of two heads, belonging, it was clear, to the men at the tiller.

'Reload,' he said to his men, remembering by a miracle to give the order. The ramrods went down the pistol barrels.

'Do that carefully if you ever want to see Pompey again,' said Hornblower.

There was a sudden crash of glass. Someone had thrust a musket barrel through the big stern window of the galley's after cabin. Luckily, having thrust it through, he had to recover himself to take aim. An irregular volley of pistols almost coincided with the report of the musket. Where the Spaniard's bullet went no one knew; but the Spaniard fell back from the window.

'By God! That's our way!' screamed Hornblower, and then, steadying himself, 'Reload.'

As the bullets were being spat into the barrels he stood up. His unused pistols were still in his belt; his cutlass was at his side.

'Come aft, here,' he said to stroke oar; the jolly-boat would stand no more weight in the bows than she had already. 'And you, too.'

Hornblower poised himself on the thwarts, eyeing the grapnel line and the cabin window.

'Bring 'em after me one at a time, Jackson,' he said.

Then he braced himself and flung himself at the grapnel line. His feet grazed the water as the line sagged, but using all his clumsy strength his arms carried him upwards. Here was the shattered window at his side; he swung up his feet, kicked out a big remaining piece of the pane, and then shot his feet through and then the rest of himself. He came down on the deck of the cabin with a thud; it was dark in here compared with the blinding sun outside. As he got to his feet, he trod on something which gave out a cry of pain – the wounded Spaniard, evidently – and the hand with which he drew his cutlass was sticky with blood. Spanish blood. Rising, he hit his head a thunderous crash on the deck-beams above, for the little cabin was very low, hardly more than five feet, and so severe was the blow that his senses

almost left him. But before him was the cabin door
and he reeled out through it, cutlass in hand. Over his
head he heard a stamping of feet, and shots were fired
behind him and above him – a further exchange, he
presumed, between the jolly-boat and the galley's stern
rail. The cabin door opened into a low half-deck, and
Hornblower reeled along it out into the sunshine again.
He was on the tiny strip of main deck at the break of the
poop. Before him stretched the narrow gangway between
the two sets of rowers; he could look down at these
latter – two seas of bearded faces, mops of hair and lean,
sunburned bodies, swinging rhythmically back and forward to the beat of the oars.

That was all the impression he could form of them at
the moment. At the far end of the gangway at the break
of the forecastle stood the overseer with his whip; he
was shouting words in rhythmic succession to the slaves –
Spanish numbers, perhaps, to give them the time. There
were three or four men on the forecastle; below them
the half-doors through the forecastle bulkhead were
hooked open, through which Hornblower could see the
two big guns illuminated by the light through the port-
holes out of which they were run almost at the water
level. The guns' crews were standing by the guns, but
numerically they were far fewer than two twenty-four
pounders would demand. Hornblower remembered
Wales's estimate of no more than thirty for a galley's
crew. The men of one gun at least had been called aft to
defend the poop against the jolly-boat's attack.

A step behind him made him leap with anxiety and
he swung round, with his cutlass ready, to meet Jackson
stumbling out of the half-deck, cutlass in hand.

'Nigh on cracked my nut,' said Jackson.

He was speaking thickly like a drunken man, and his

words were chorused by further shots fired from the poop at the level of the top of their heads.

'Oldroyd's comin' next,' said Jackson. 'Franklin's dead.'

On either side of them a companion ladder mounted to the poop deck. It seemed logical, mathematical, that they should each go up one, but Hornblower thought better of it.

'Come along,' he said, and headed for the starboard ladder, and, with Oldroyd putting in an appearance at that moment, he yelled to him to follow.

The hand-ropes of the ladder were of twisted red and yellow cord – he even could notice that as he rushed up the ladder, pistol in hand and cutlass in the other. After the first step, his eye was above deck level. There were more than a dozen men crowded on the tiny poop, but two were lying dead, and one was groaning with his back to the rail, and two stood by the tiller. The others were looking over the rail at the jolly-boat. Hornblower was still insane with fighting madness. He must have leaped up the final two or three steps with a bound like a stag's, and he was screaming like a maniac as he flung himself at the Spaniards. His pistol went off apparently without his willing it, but the face of the man a yard away dissolved into bloody ruin, and Hornblower dropped the weapon and snatched the second, his thumb going to the hammer as he whirled his cutlass down with a crash on the sword which the next Spaniard raised as a feeble guard. He struck and struck and struck with a lunatic's strength. Here was Jackson beside him shouting hoarsely and striking out right and left.

'Kill 'em! Kill 'em!' shouted Jackson.

Hornblower saw Jackson's cutlass flash down on the head of the defenceless man at the tiller. Then out of

the tail of his eye he saw another sword threaten him as
he battered with his cutlass at the man before him, but
his pistol saved him as he fired automatically again.
Another pistol went off beside him – Oldroyd's, he
supposed – and then the fight on the poop was over. By
what miracle of ineptitude the Spaniards had allowed
the attack to take them by surprise Hornblower never
could discover. Perhaps they were ignorant of the wound-
ing of the man in the cabin, and had relied on him to
defend that route; perhaps it had never occurred to
them that three men could be so utterly desperate as to
attack a dozen; perhaps they never realized that three
men had made the perilous passage of the grapnel line;
perhaps – most probably – in the mad excitement of it
all, they simply lost their heads, for five minutes could
hardly have elapsed altogether from the time the jolly-
boat hooked on until the poop was cleared. Two or three
Spaniards ran down the companion to the main deck,
and forward along the gangway between the rows of
slaves. One was caught against the rail and made a
gesture of surrender, but Jackson's hand was already at
his throat. Jackson was a man of immense physical
strength; he bent the Spaniard back over the rail, farther
and farther, and then caught him by the thigh with his
other hand and heaved him over. He fell with a shriek
before Hornblower could interpose. The poop deck was
covered with writhing men, like the bottom of a boat
filled with flapping fish. One man was getting to his
knees when Jackson and Oldroyd seized him. They swung
him up to toss him over the rail.

'Stop that!' said Hornblower, and quite callously they
dropped him again with a crash on the bloody planks.

Jackson and Oldroyd were like drunken men, unsteady
on their feet, glazed of eye and stertorous of breath;

Hornblower was just coming out of his insane fit. He stepped forward to the break of the poop, wiping the sweat out of his eyes while trying to wipe away the red mist that tinged his vision. Forward by the forecastle were gathered the rest of the Spaniards, a large group of them; as Hornblower came forward, one of them fired a musket at him, but the ball went wide. Down below him the rowers were still swinging rhythmically, forward and back, forward and back, the hairy heads and the naked bodies moving in time to the oars; in time to the voice of the overseer, too, for the latter was still standing on the gangway (the rest of the Spaniards were clustered behind him) calling the time – '*Seis, siete, ocho.*'

'Stop!' bellowed Hornblower.

He walked to the starboard side to be in full view of the starboard side rowers. He held up his hand and bellowed again. A hairy face or two was raised, but the oars still swung.

'*Uno, doce, tres,*' said the overseer.

Jackson appeared at Hornblower's elbow, and levelled a pistol to shoot the nearest rower.

'Oh, belay that!' said Hornblower testily. He knew he was sick of killings now. 'Find my pistols and reload them.'

He stood at the top of the companion like a man in a dream – in a nightmare. The galley slaves went on swinging and pulling; his dozen enemies were still clustered at the break of the forecastle thirty yards away; behind him the wounded Spaniards groaned away their lives. Another appeal to the rowers was as much ignored as the preceding ones. Oldroyd must have had the clearest head or have recovered himself quickest.

'I'll haul down his colours, sir, shall I?' he said.

Hornblower woke from his dream. On a staff above the taffrail fluttered the yellow and red.

'Yes, haul 'em down at once,' he said.

Now his mind was clear, and now his horizon was no longer bounded by the narrow limits of the galley. He looked about him, over the blue, blue sea. There were the merchant ships; over there lay the *Indefatigable*. Behind him boiled the white wake of the galley – a curved wake. Not until that moment did he realize that he was in control of the tiller, and that for the last three minutes, the galley had been cutting over the blue seas unsteered.

'Take the tiller, Oldroyd,' he ordered.

Was that a galley disappearing into the hazy distance? It must be, and far in its wake was the long-boat. And there, on the port bow, was the gig, resting on her oars – Hornblower could see little figures standing waving in bow and stern, and it dawned upon him that this was in acknowledgment of the hauling down of the Spanish colours. Another musket banged off forward, and the rail close at his hip was struck a tremendous blow which sent gilded splinters flying in the sunlight. But he had all his wits about him again, and he ran back over the dying men; at the after end of the poop he was out of sight of the gangway and safe from shot. He could still see the gig on the port bow.

'Starboard your helm, Oldroyd.'

The galley turned slowly – her narrow length made her unhandy if the rudder were not assisted by the oars – but soon the bow was about to obscure the gig.

'Midships!'

Amazing that there, leaping in the white water that boiled under the galley's stern, was the jolly-boat with one live man and two dead men still aboard.

'Where are the others, Bromley?' yelled Jackson.

Bromley pointed overside. They had been shot from the taffrail at the moment that Hornblower and the others were preparing to attack the poop.

'Why in hell don't you come aboard?'

Bromley took hold of his left arm with his right; the limb was clearly useless. There was no reinforcement to be obtained here, and yet full possession must be taken of the galley. Otherwise it was even conceivable that they would be carried off to Algeciras; even if they were masters of the rudder the man who controlled the oars dictated the course of the ship if he willed. There was only one course left to try.

Now that his fighting madness had ebbed away, Hornblower was in a sombre mood. He did not care what happened to him; hope and fear had alike deserted him, along with his previous exalted condition. It might be resignation that possessed him now. His mind, still calculating, told him that with only one thing left to do to achieve victory he must attempt it, and the flat, dead condition of his spirits enabled him to carry the attempt through like an automaton, unwavering and emotionless. He walked forward to the poop rail again; the Spaniards were still clustered at the far end of the gangway, with the overseer still giving the time to the oars. They looked up at him as he stood there. With the utmost care and attention he sheathed his cutlass, which he had held in his hand up to that moment. He noticed the blood on his coat and on his hands as he did so. Slowly he settled the sheathed weapon at his side.

'My pistols, Jackson,' he said.

Jackson handed him the pistols and with the same callous care he thrust them into his belt. He turned back to Oldroyd, the Spaniards watching every movement fascinated.

'Stay by the tiller, Oldroyd. Jackson, follow me. Do nothing without my orders.'

With the sun pouring down on his face, he strode down the companion ladder, walked to the gangway, and approached the Spaniards along it. On either side of him the hairy heads and naked bodies of the galley slaves still swung with the oars. He neared the Spaniards; swords and muskets and pistols were handled nervously, but every eye was on his face. Behind him Jackson coughed. Two yards only from the group, Hornblower halted and swept them with his glance. Then, with a gesture, he indicated the whole of the group except the overseer; and then pointed to the forecastle.

'Get forrard, all of you,' he said.

They stood staring at him, although they must have understood the gesture.

'Get forrard,' said Hornblower with a wave of his hand and a tap of his foot on the gangway.

There was only one man who seemed likely to demur actively, and Hornblower had it in mind to snatch a pistol from his belt and shoot him on the spot. But the pistol might misfire, the shot might arouse the Spaniards out of their fascinated dream. He stared the man down.

'Get forrard, I say.'

They began to move, they began to shamble off. Hornblower watched them go. Now his emotions were returning to him, and his heart was thumping madly in his chest so that it was hard to control himself. Yet he must not be precipitate. He had to wait until the others were well clear before he could address himself to the overseer.

'Stop those men,' he said.

He glared into the overseer's eyes while pointing to

the oarsmen; the overseer's lips moved, but he made no sound.

'Stop them,' said Hornblower, and this time he put his hand to the butt of his pistol.

That sufficed. The overseer raised his voice in a high-pitched order, and the oars instantly ceased. Strange what sudden stillness possessed the ship with the cessation of the grinding of the oars in the tholes. Now it was easy to hear the bubbling of the water round the galley as her way carried her forward. Hornblower turned back to hail Oldroyd.

'Oldroyd! Where away's the gig?'

'Close on the starboard bow, sir!'

'How close?'

'Two cable's length, sir. She's pulling for us now.'

'Steer for her while you've steerage way.'

'Aye aye, sir.'

How long would it take the gig under oars to cover a quarter of a mile? Hornblower feared anticlimax, feared a sudden revulsion of feeling among the Spaniards at this late moment. Mere waiting might occasion it, and he must not stand merely idle. He could still hear the motion of the galley through the water, and he turned to Jackson.

'This ship carries her way well, Jackson, doesn't she?' he said, and he made himself laugh as he spoke, as if everything in the world was a matter of sublime certainty.

'Aye, sir, I suppose she does, sir,' said the startled Jackson; he was fidgeting nervously with his pistols.

'And look at the man there,' went on Hornblower, pointing to a galley slave. 'Did you ever see such a beard in your life?'

'N-no, sir.'

'Speak to me, you fool. Talk naturally.'

'I – I dunno what to say, sir.'

'You've no sense, damn you, Jackson. See the welt on that fellow's shoulder? He must have caught it from the overseer's whip not so long ago.'

'Mebbe you're right, sir.'

Hornblower was repressing his impatience and was about to make another speech when he heard a rasping thump alongside and a moment later the gig's crew was pouring over the bulwarks. The relief was inexpressible. Hornblower was about to relax completely when he remembered appearances. He stiffened himself up.

'Glad to see you aboard, sir,' he said, as Lieutenant Chadd swung his legs over and dropped to the main deck at the break of the forecastle.

'Glad to see *you*,' said Chadd, looking about him curiously.

'These men forrard are prisoners, sir,' said Hornblower. 'It might be well to secure them. I think that is all that remains to be done.'

Now he could not relax; it seemed to him as if he must remain strained and tense for ever. Strained and yet stupid, even when he heard the cheers of the hands in the *Indefatigable* as the galley came alongside her. Stupid and dull, making a stumbling report to Captain Pellew, forcing himself to remember to commend the bravery of Jackson and Oldroyd in the highest terms.

'The Admiral will be pleased,' said Pellew, looking at Hornblower keenly.

'I'm glad, sir,' Hornblower heard himself say.

'Now that we've lost poor Soames,' went on Pellew, 'we shall need another watch-keeping officer. I have it in mind to give you an order as acting-lieutenant.'

'Thank you, sir,' said Hornblower, still stupid.

Soames had been a grey-haired officer of vast experience. He had sailed the seven seas, he had fought in a score of actions. But, faced with a new situation, he had not had the quickness of thought to keep his boat from under the ram of the galley. Soames was dead, and acting-lieutenant Hornblower would take his place. Fighting madness, sheer insanity, had won him this promise of promotion. Hornblower had never realized the black depths of lunacy into which he could sink. Like Soames, like all the rest of the crew of the *Indefatigable*, he had allowed himself to be carried away by his blind hatred for the galleys, and only good fortune had allowed him to live through it. That was something worth remembering.

An Attack that Failed

Lieutenant William Bush first made Hornblower's acquaintance in H.M.S. Renown, *a seventy-four gun ship of the line to which both were appointed as lieutenants in 1800, several years after the capture of the Spanish galley. Hornblower had spent much of the interim in a Spanish prison. Bush, who was the senior by twelve months, found himself the* Renown's *third lieutenant, while Hornblower was the fifth and junior. It was during this commission that Bush, who was to share many of Hornblower's adventures in years to come, learnt to recognize the outstanding ability of his younger messmate.*

The Renown *had sailed to join the British squadron in the West Indies soon after Bush joined her, and he quickly discovered that she was an unhappy and unfortunate ship. Captain Sawyer was a man of curious temperament who took it into his head to suspect all his officers of plotting against him, of trying to undermine his authority, even of mutiny. He read into their most innocent actions and remarks evidence of deepest villainy, and inflicted on them such monstrous punishments as that of ordering them to report fully dressed to Mr Buckland, the first lieutenant, once every hour throughout day and night, which allowed neither them nor the first lieutenant any opportunity for proper sleep.*

Matters grew worse during the long transatlantic crossing until the captain was clearly no longer in his right mind, and the officers were driven very reluctantly to do the very thing he had been falsely accusing them of – to plan secretly among themselves how they could deprive him of command. But the captain got wind of their midnight meeting and called out the marine guard to arrest them. Then, by a strange, providential stroke of fortune, he tumbled down a hatchway and was discovered by Hornblower, a few minutes later, lying unconscious at the foot of the ladder. The accident not only gave the officers time to break up their meeting and escape but also the excuse to confine the captain to his cabin under the surgeon's care.

Among the officers there was a suspicion that the captain's fall which thus saved them from their difficulties was too timely to have been entirely accidental, and they looked to Hornblower for some explanation, not only because he had been the first to reach the scene, but also because they instinctively felt that he alone among them was resourceful enough to have contrived so neat a way out of a desperate situation. In spite of Hornblower's denial of knowing any more than they, the suspicion remained and they were inclined to give to him, in their own minds, the credit for having saved them.

Their troubles were by no means over. With the captain incapacitated, the drastic step of depriving him of his command on the grounds of insanity was easier to take, and Buckland, as second-in-command, was persuaded to do it. It was a momentous decision; the captain of one of His Majesty's ships held his command under the authority of the King himself and could not be removed except under the most exceptional circumstances. To declare him unfit to command was an act that would have to be completely justified, as soon as the Renown joined the fleet, before a court of inquiry. If Captain Sawyer recovered, as well he might before the voyage ended, and charged his officers with mutinous conduct, they might all be hanging from the yard-arm the following day.

In the atmosphere of hesitation and uneasiness that per-

vaded the wardroom, Bush was quick to notice the quiet and apparently untroubled determination of Hornblower's manner. He alone seemed able to think logically and act wisely. He had been largely instrumental, Bush was sure, in persuading Buckland to assume command and to search the captain's desk for the secret orders under which they were sailing.

These orders required the Renown, *before proceeding to Kingston, Jamaica, and placing herself under the admiral commanding the West Indian squadron, to make for the island of Santo Domingo, or Haiti as it was sometimes called, and to destroy the nest of Spanish privateers based on Samaná Bay which preyed on the British merchant shipping using the near-by Mona Passage. Buckland was neither a brilliant officer nor a resolute character; heavy responsibilities had been suddenly thrust on him at a time when he was still suffering from the anxiety and physical exhaustion caused by the captain's behaviour. He was tempted to rid himself of them as soon as possible by sailing straight to Jamaica, but he was prevailed upon – by Hornblower, Bush again suspected – to follow the orders and take the privateers first.*

LIEUTENANT BUCKLAND, in acting command of H.M.S. *Renown*, of seventy-four guns, was on the quarter-deck of his ship peering through his telescope at the low mountains of Santo Domingo. The ship was rolling in a fashion unnatural and disturbing, for the long Atlantic swell, driven by the north-east trades, was passing under her keel while she lay hove-to to the final puffs of the land breeze which had blown since midnight and was now dying away as the fierce sun heated the island again. The *Renown* was actually wallowing, rolling her lower-deck gunports under, first on one side and then on the other, for what little breeze there was was along the swell and did nothing to stiffen her as she lay with her mizen topsail backed. She would lie right over on one side, until the gun tackles creaked with the strain of holding the guns in position, until it was hard to keep a foothold on the steep-sloping deck; she would lie there for a few harrowing seconds, and then slowly right herself, making no pause at all at the moment when she was upright and her deck horizontal, and continue, with a clattering of blocks and a rattle of gear in a sickening swoop until she was as far over in the opposite direction, gun tackles creaking and unwary men slipping and sliding, and lie there unresponsive until the swell had rolled under her and she repeated her behaviour.

'For God's sake,' said Hornblower, hanging on to a belaying pin in the mizen fife rail to save himself from sliding down the deck into the scuppers, 'can't he make up his mind?'

There was something in Hornblower's stare that made Bush look at him more closely.

'Seasick?' he asked, with curiosity.

'Who wouldn't be?' replied Hornblower. 'How she rolls!'

Bush's cast-iron stomach had never given him the least qualm, but he was aware that less fortunate men suffered from seasickness even after weeks at sea, especially when subjected to a different kind of motion. This funereal rolling was nothing like the free action of the *Renown* under sail.

'Buckland has to see how the land lies,' he said in an effort to cheer Hornblower up.

'How much more does he want to see?' grumbled

Hornblower. 'There's the Spanish colours flying on the fort up there. Everyone on shore knows now that a ship of the line is prowling about, and the Dons won't have to be very clever to guess that we're not here on a yachting trip. Now they've all the time they need to be ready to receive us.'

'But what else could he do?'

'He could have come in in the dark with the sea breeze. Landing parties ready. Put them ashore at dawn. Storm the place before they knew there was any danger. Oh, God!'

The final exclamation had nothing to do with what went before. It was wrenched out of Hornblower by the commotion of his stomach. Despite his deep tan there was a sickly green colour in his cheeks.

'Hard luck,' said Bush.

Buckland still stood trying to keep his telescope trained on the coast despite the rolling of the ship. This was Scotchman's Bay – the Bahia de Escocesa, as the Spanish charts had it. To the westward lay a shelving beach; the big rollers here broke far out and ran in creamy white up to the water's edge with diminishing force, but to the eastward the shore line rose in a line of tree-covered hills standing bluffly with their feet in blue water; the rollers burst against them in sheets of spray that climbed far up the cliffs before falling back in a smother of white. For thirty miles those hills ran beside the sea, almost due east and west; they constituted the Samaná peninsula, terminating in Samaná Point. According to the charts the peninsula was no more than ten miles wide; behind them, round Samaná Point, lay Samaná Bay, opening into the Mona Passage and a most convenient anchorage for privateers and small ships of war.

The main topsail suddenly flapped like thunder, and the

ship began to turn slowly head to sea; the land breeze was expiring, and the trade winds, blowing eternally across the Atlantic, were resuming their dominion. Buckland shut his telescope with relief. At least that was an excuse for postponing action.

'Mr Roberts!'

'Sir!'

'Lay her on the port tack. Full and by!'

'Aye aye, sir.'

The after guard came running to the mizen braces, and the ship slowly paid off. Gradually the topsails caught the wind, and she began to lie over, gathering way as she did so. She met the next roller with her port bow, thrusting boldly into it in a burst of spray. The tautened weather-rigging began to sing a more cheerful note, blending with the music of her passage through the water. She was a live thing again, instead of rolling like a corpse in the trough. The roaring trade wind pressed her over, and she went surging along, rising and swooping as if with pleasure, leaving a creamy wake behind her on the blue water while the sea roared under the bows.

'Better?' asked Bush of Hornblower.

'Better in one way,' was the reply. Hornblower looked over at the distant hills of Santo Domingo. 'I could wish we were going into action and not running away to think about it.'

'What a fire-eater!' said Bush.

'A fire-eater? Me? Nothing like that – quite the opposite. I wish – oh, I wish for too much, I suppose.'

There was no explaining some people, thought Bush, philosophically. He was content to bask in the sunshine now that its heat was tempered by the ship's passage through the wind. If action and danger lay in the future he could await it in stolid tranquillity; and he certainly could congratulate himself that he did not have to carry Buckland's responsibility of carrying a ship of the line and seven hundred and twenty men into action. The prospect of action at least took one's mind off the horrid fact that confined below lay an insane captain.

At dinner in the wardroom he looked over at Hornblower, fidgety and nervous. Buckland had announced his intention of taking the bull by the horns the next morning, of rounding Samaná Point and forcing his way straight up the bay. It would not take many broadsides from the *Renown* to destroy any shipping that lay there at anchor. Bush thoroughly approved of the scheme. Wipe out the privateers, burn them, sink them, and then it would be time to decide what, if anything, should be done next.

Half-way through next morning the pipes shrilled along the decks; the drums of the marines beat a rousing roll.

'Clear the decks for action! Hands to quarters! Clear for action!'

Bush came down to the lower gun-deck, which was his station for action; under his command was the whole deck and the seventeen twenty-four-pounders of the starboard battery, while Hornblower commanded under him those of the port side.

Hornblower made his appearance, touched his hat to Bush, and stood by to supervise his guns. Most of this lower deck was in twilight, for the stout shafts of sunlight that came down the hatchways did little to illuminate the farther parts of the deck with its sombre red paint. Half a dozen ship's boys came along, each one carrying a bucket of sand, which they scattered in handfuls over the deck. Bush kept a sharp eye on them, because the guns' crews depended on that sand for firm foothold. The water buckets beside each gun were filled; they served a dual purpose, to dampen the swabs that cleaned out the guns and for immediate use against fire. Round the mainmast stood a ring of extra fire buckets; in tubs at either side of the ship smouldered the slow matches from which the gun captains could rekindle their linstocks when necessary. Fire and water. The marine sentries came clumping along the deck in their scarlet coats and white crossbelts, the tops of their shakos brushing the deck beams over their heads. Corporal Greenwood posted one at each hatchway, bayonet fixed and musket loaded. Their duty was to see that no unauthorized person ran down to take shelter in the safety of that part of the ship comfortably below waterline. Mr Hobbs, the acting-gunner, with his mates and helpers made a momentary appearance on their way down to the magazine. They were all wearing list slippers to obviate any chance of setting off loose powder which would be bound to be strewn about down there in the heat of action.

Soon the powder boys came running up, each with a charge for the guns. The breechings of the guns were cast off and the crews stood by the tackles, waiting for the word to open the ports and run out the guns. Bush darted his glance along both sides. The gun captains were all at their posts. Ten men stood by every gun on the starboard side, five by every gun on the port side – maximum and minimum crews for twenty-four-pounders. It was Bush's responsibility to see to it that whichever battery came into action the guns were properly manned. If both sides had to be worked at once he had to make a fair division, and when the casualties began and guns were put out of service he had to redistribute the crews. The petty officers and warrant officers were reporting their subdivisions ready for action, and Bush turned to the midshipman beside him whose duty was to carry messages.

'Mr Abbott, report the lower deck cleared for action. Ask if the guns should be run out.'

'Aye aye, sir.'

Silently the ship sailed on; even Bush had his ears cocked, trying to hear what was going on above him so as to draw deductions about the situation. Faintly down the hatchway came the call of a seaman.

'No bottom, sir. No bottom with this line.'

So there was a man in the chains taking casts with the lead, and they must be drawing near the land. Now a midshipman appeared descending the ladder.

'Mr Buckland's compliments, sir, and please to run your guns out.'

He had squealed his message without ever setting foot on deck, and everyone had heard it. There was an instant buzz round the deck, and excitable people began to reach for the gunports to open them.

'Still!' bellowed Bush. Guiltily all movement ceased.

'Up ports!'

The twilight of the lower deck changed to daylight as the ports opened; little rectangles of sunshine swayed about on the deck on the port side, broadening and narrowing with the motion of the ship.

'Run out!'

With the ports open the noise was not so great; the crews flung their weight on the tackles and the trucks roared as the guns thrust their muzzles out. Bush stepped to the nearest gun and stooped to peer out through the open port. There were the green hills of the island at extreme gunshot distance; here the cliffs were not nearly so abrupt, and there was a jungle-covered shelf at their feet.

'Hands wear ship!'

Bush could recognize Roberts' voice hailing from the quarter-deck. The deck under his feet steadied to the horizontal, and the distant hills seemed to swing with the vessel. The masts creaked as the yards came round. That must be Samaná Point which they were rounding. The motion of the ship had changed far more than would be the result of mere alteration of course. She was not only on an even keel but she was in quiet water, gliding along into the bay. Bush squatted down on his heels by the muzzle of a gun and peered at the shore. This was the south side of the peninsula at which he was looking, presenting a coastline towards the bay nearly as steep as the one on the seaward side. There was the fort on the crest and the Spanish flag waving over it. The excited midshipman came scuttling down the ladder like a squirrel.

'Sir! Sir! Will you try a ranging shot at the batteries when your guns bear?'

Bush ran a cold eye over him.

'Whose orders?' he asked.

'M – Mr Buckland's, sir.'

'Then say so. Very well. My respect to Mr Buckland, and it will be a long time before my guns are within range.'

'Aye aye, sir.'

There was smoke rising from the fort, and not powder smoke either. Bush realized with something like a quiver of apprehension that probably it was smoke from a furnace for heating shot; soon the fort would be hurling red-hot shot at them, and Bush could see no chance of retaliation; he would never be able to elevate his guns sufficiently to reach the fort, while the fort, from its commanding position on the crest, could reach the ship easily enough. He straightened himself up and walked over to the port side to where Hornblower, in a similar attitude, was peering out beside a gun.

'There's a point running out here,' said Hornblower. 'See the shallows there? The channel must bend round them. And there's a battery on the point – look at the smoke. They're heating shot.'

'I dare say,' said Bush.

Soon they would be under a sharp crossfire. He hoped they would not be subjected to it for too long. He could hear orders being shouted on deck, and the masts creaked as the yards came round; they were working the *Renown* round the bend.

'The fort's opened fire, sir,' reported the master's mate in charge of the forward guns on the starboard side.

'Very well, Mr Purvis.' He crossed over and looked out. 'Did you see where the shot fell?'

'No, sir.'

'They're firing on this side, too, sir,' reported Hornblower.

'Very well.'

Bush saw the fort spurting white cannon smoke. Then straight in the line between his eye and the fort, fifty yards from the side of the ship, a pillar of water rose up from the golden surface, and within the same instant of time something crashed into the side of the ship just above Bush's head. A ricochet had bounded from the surface and had lodged somewhere in the eighteen inches of oak that constituted the ship's side. Then followed a devil's tattoo of crashes; a well-aimed salvo was striking home.

'I might just reach the battery on this side now, sir,' said Hornblower.

'Then try what you can do.'

They were working the Renown *round the bend*

Now here was Buckland himself, hailing fretfully down the hatchway.

'Can't you open fire yet, Mr Bush?'

'This minute, sir.'

Hornblower was standing by the centre twenty-four-pounder. The gun captain slid the rolling handspite under the gun carriage, and heaved with all his weight. Two men at each side tackle tugged under his direction to point the gun true. With the elevating coign quite free from the breech the gun was at its highest angle of elevation. The gun captain flipped up the iron apron over the touchhole, saw that the hole was filled with powder, and with a shout of 'Stand clear', he thrust his smouldering linstock into it. The gun bellowed loud in the confined space; some of the smoke came drifting back through the port.

'Just below, sir,' reported Hornblower, standing at the next port. 'When the guns are hot they'll reach it.'

'Carry on, then.'

'Open fire, first division!' yelled Hornblower.

The four foremost guns crashed out almost together.

'Second division!'

Bush could feel the deck heaving under him with the shock of the discharge and the recoil. Smoke came billowing back into the confined space, acrid, bitter; and the din was paralysing.

'Try again, men!' yelled Hornblower. 'Division captains, see that you point true!'

There was a frightful crash close beside Bush and something screamed past him to crash into the deck beam near his head. Something flying through an open gunport had struck a gun on its reinforced breech. Two men had fallen close beside it, one lying still and the other twisting and turning in agony. Bush was about to give an order regarding them when his attention was drawn to something more important. There was a deep gash in the deck beam by his head and from the depths of the gash smoke was curling. It was a red-hot shot that had struck the breech of the gun and had apparently flown into fragments. A large part – the largest part – had sunk deep into the beam and already the wood was smouldering.

'Fire buckets here!' roared Bush.

Ten pounds of red-hot glowing metal lodged in the dry timbers of the ship could start a blaze in a few seconds. At the same time there was a rush of feet overhead, the sound of gear being moved about, and then the clank-clank of pumps. So on the main deck they were fighting fires, too. Hornblower's guns were thundering on the port side, the gun-trucks roaring over the planking. Hell was unchained, and the smoke of hell was eddying about him.

The masts creaked again with the swing of the yards; despite everything the ship had to be sailed up the tortuous channel. He peered out through a port, but his eye told him, as he forced himself to gauge the distance calmly, that the fort on the crest was still beyond range. No sense in wasting ammunition. He straightened himself and looked round the murky deck. There was something strange in the feel of the ship under his feet. He teetered on his toes to put his wild suspicions to the test. There was the slightest perceptible slope to the deck – a strange rigidity and permanence about it. Oh, my God! Hornblower was looking round at him and making an urgent gesture downwards to confirm the awful thought. The *Renown* was aground. She must have run so smoothly and slowly up a mudbank as to lose her speed without any jerk perceptible. But she must have put her bows far up on the bank for the slope of the deck to be noticeable. There were more rending crashes as other shots from the shore struck home, a fresh hurrying and bustle as the fire parties ran to deal with the danger. Hard aground, and doomed to be slowly shot to pieces by those cursed forts, if the shots did not set them on fire to roast alive on the mudbank. Hornblower was beside him, his watch in his hand.

'Tide's still rising,' he said. 'It's an hour before high water. But I'm afraid we're pretty hard aground.'

'An hour to high water, you say?' he asked.

'Yes, sir. According to Carberry's calculations.'

'God help us!'

'My shot's just reaching the battery on that point, sir. If I can keep the embrasures swept I'll slow their rate of fire even if I don't silence them.'

Another crash as a shot struck home, and another.

'But the one across the channel's out of range.'

'Yes,' said Hornblower.

The powder boys were running through all the bustle with fresh charges for the guns. And here was the messenger-midshipman threading his way through them.

'Mr Bush, sir! Will you please report to Mr Buckland, sir? And we're aground, under fire, sir.'

'Shut your mouth. I leave you in charge here, Mr Hornblower.'

'Aye aye, sir.'

The sunlight on the quarter-deck was blinding. Buckland was standing hatless at the rail, trying to control the working of his features. There was a roar and a spluttering of steam as someone turned the jet of a hose on a fiery fragment lodged in the bulkhead. Dead men in the scuppers; wounded being carried off. A shot, or the splinters it had sent flying, must have killed the man at the wheel so that the ship, temporarily out of control, had run aground.

'We'll have to kedge off,' said Buckland.

'Aye aye, sir.'

That meant putting out an anchor and heaving in on the cable with the capstan to haul the ship off the mud by main force. Bush looked round him to confirm what he had gathered regarding the ship's position from his restricted view below. Her bows were on the mud; she would have to be hauled off stern first. A shot howled close overhead, and Bush had to exert his self-control not to jump.

'You'll have to get a cable out aft through a stern port.'

'Aye aye, sir.'

'Roberts'll take the stream anchor off in the launch.'

'Aye aye, sir.'

The fact that Buckland omitted the formal 'Mister' was significant of the strain he was undergoing and of the emergency of the occasion.

'I'll take the men from my guns, sir,' said Bush.

'Very good.'

Bush gathered his guns' crews around him and set about the task of rousing out a cable and getting it aft to a port, while overhead Roberts' men were manning stay tackles and yard tackles to sway out the launch.

Down below the heat between the decks was greater even than above with the sun glaring down. The smoke from Hornblower's guns was eddying thick under the beams; Hornblower was holding his hat in his hand and wiping his streaming face with his handkerchief. He nodded as Bush appeared; there was no need for Bush to explain the duty on which he was engaged. With the guns still thundering and the smoke still eddying, powder boys still running with fresh charges and fire parties bustling with their buckets, Bush's men roused out the cable. The hundred fathoms of it weighed a trifle over a couple of tons; clear heads and skilled supervision were necessary to get the unwieldy cable laid out aft, but Bush was at his best doing work which called for single-minded attention to a single duty. He had it clear and faked down along the deck by the time the cutter was under the stern to receive the end, and then he watched the vast thing gradually snake out through the after port without a hitch. The launch came into his line of vision as he stood looking out, with the vast weight of the stream anchor dangling astern; it was a relief to know that the tricky business of getting the anchor into her had been successfully carried out. The second cutter carried the spring cable from the hawse-hole. Roberts was in command; Bush heard him hail the cutter as the three boats drew off astern. There was a sudden jet of water among the boats; one or other, if not both, of the batteries ashore had shifted target; a shot now into the launch would be a disaster, and one into a cutter would be a serious setback.

'Pardon, sir,' said Hornblower's voice beside him, and Bush turned back from looking out over the glittering water.

'Well?'

'I could take some of the foremost guns and run 'em aft,' said Hornblower. 'Shifting the weight would help.'

'So it would,' agreed Bush; Hornblower's face was streaked and grimy with his exertions, as Bush noted while he considered if he had sufficient authority to give the order on his own responsibility. 'Better get Buckland's permission. Ask him in my name if you like.'

'Aye aye, sir.'

These lower-deck twenty-four-pounders weighed more than two tons each; the transfer of some from forward aft would be an important factor in getting the bows off the mudbank. Bush took another glance through the port. James, the midshipman in the first cutter, was turning to look back to check that the cable was out in exact line with the length of the ship. There would be a serious loss of tractive effort if there was an angle in the cable from anchor to capstan. Launch and cutter were coming together in preparation for dropping the anchor. All round them the water suddenly boiled to a salvo from the shore; the skipping jets of the ricochets showed that it was the fort on the hill that was firing at them – and making good practice for that extreme range. The sun caught an axe blade as it turned in the air in the sternsheets of the launch; Bush saw the momentary flash. They were letting the anchor drop from where it hung from the gallows in the stern. Thank God.

Hornblower's guns were still bellowing out, making the ship tremble with their recoil, and at the same time a splintering crash over his head told him that the other battery was still firing on the ship and still scoring hits. Everything was still going on at once; Hornblower had a gang of men at work dragging aft the foremost twenty-four-pounder on the starboard side – a ticklish job with the rolling handspike under the transom of the carriage. The trucks squealed horribly as the men struggled to turn the cumbersome thing and thread their way along the crowded deck. But Bush could spare Hornblower no more than a glance as he hurried up to the main deck to see for himself what was happening at the capstan.

The men were already taking their places at the capstan bars under the supervision of Smith and Booth; the main deck guns were being stripped of the last of their crews to supply enough hands. Naked to the waist, the men were spitting on their hands and testing their foothold – there was no need to tell them how serious the situation was; no need for Booth's knotted rattan.

'Heave away!' hailed Buckland from the quarter-deck.

'Heave away!' yelled Booth. 'Heave, and wake the dead!'

The men flung their weights on the bars and the capstan came round, the pawls clanking rapidly as the capstan took up the slack. Then the intervals between the clanking of the pawls became longer as the capstan turned more slowly. More slowly; clank – clank – clank. Now the strain was coming; the bitts creaked as the cable tightened. Clank – clank. That was a new cable, and it could be expected to stretch a trifle.

'Heave!' shouted Booth. Clank – clank – clank. Slowly and more slowly still turned the capstan. Then it came to a dead stop while the bitts groaned under the strain.

'Heave! Heave!'

Clank! Then reluctantly, and after a long interval, clank! Then no more. The merciless sun beat down upon the men's straining backs; their horny feet sought for a grip against the cleats on the deck as they shoved and thrust against the bars. Bush went below again, leaving them straining away; he could, and did, send plenty of men up from the lower gun-deck to treble-bank the capstan bars. There were men still hard at work in the smoky twilight hauling the last possible gun aft, but Hornblower was back among his guns supervising the pointing. Bush set his foot on the cable. It was not like a rope, but like a wooden spar, as rigid and unyielding. Then through the sole of his shoe Bush felt the slightest tremor, the very slightest; the men at the capstan were putting their reinforced strength against the bars. The clank of one more pawl gained reverberated along the ship's timbers; the cable shuddered a trifle more violently and then stiffened into total rigidity again. It did not creep over an eighth of an inch under Bush's foot, although he knew that at the capstan a hundred and fifty men were straining their hearts out at the bars. One of Hornblower's guns went off; Bush felt the jar of the recoil through the cable. Faintly down the hatchways came the shouts of encouragement from Smith and Booth at the capstan, but not an inch of gain could be noted at the cable. Hornblower came and touched his hat to Bush.

'D'you notice any movement when I fire a gun, sir?' As he asked the question he turned and waved to the captain of a midship gun which was loaded and run out. The gun captain brought the linstock down on the touchhole, and the gun roared out and came recoiling back through the smoke. Bush's foot on the cable recorded the effect.

'Only the jar – no – yes.' Inspiration came to Bush. To the question he asked, Bush already knew the answer Hornblower would give. 'What are you thinking of?'

'I could fire all my guns at once. That might break the suction, sir.'

So it might, indeed. The *Renown* was lying on mud, which was clutching her in a firm grip. If she could be severely shaken while the hawser was maintained at full tension the grip might be broken.

'I think it's worth trying, by God,' said Bush.

'Very good, sir. I'll have my guns loaded and ready in three minutes, sir.' Hornblower turned to his battery and funnelled his hands round his mouth. 'Cease fire! Cease fire, all!'

'I'll tell 'em at the capstan,' said Bush.

'Very good, sir.' Hornblower went on giving his orders. 'Load and double-shot your guns. Prime and run out.'

That was the last that Bush heard for the moment as he

went up on the main deck and made his suggestion to Smith, who nodded in instant agreement.

''Vast heaving!' shouted Smith, and the sweating men at the bars eased their weary backs.

An explanation was necessary to Buckland on the quarter-deck; he saw the force of the argument. The unfortunate man, who was watching the failure of his first venture in independent command, and whose ship was in such deadly peril, was gripping at the rail and wringing it with his two hands as if he would twist it like a corkscrew. In the midst of all this there was a piece of desperately important news that Smith had to give.

'Roberts is dead,' he said, out of the side of his mouth.

'No!'

'He's dead. A shot cut him in two in the launch.'

'Good God!'

It was to Bush's credit that he felt sorrow at the death of Roberts before his mind recorded the fact that he was now first lieutenant of a ship of the line. But there was no time now to think of either sorrow or rejoicing, not with the *Renown* aground and under fire. Bush hailed down the hatchway.

'Below, there! Mr Hornblower!'

'Sir!'

'Are your guns ready?'

'Another minute, sir.'

'Better take the strain,' said Bush to Smith; and then, louder, down the hatchway, 'Await my order, Mr Hornblower.'

'Aye aye, sir.'

The men settled themselves at the capstan bars again, braced their feet, and heaved.

'Heave!' shouted Booth. 'Heave!'

The men might be pushing at the side of a church, so little movement did they get from the bars after the first inch.

'Heave!'

Bush left them and ran below. He set his foot on the rigid cable and nodded to Hornblower. The fifteen guns – two had been dragged aft from the port side – were run out and ready, the crews awaiting orders.

'Captains, take your linstocks!' shouted Hornblower. 'All you others, stand clear! Now, I shall give you the words "one, two, three." At "three" you touch your linstocks down. Understand?'

There was a buzz of agreement.

'All ready? All linstocks glowing?' The gun captains swung them about to get them as bright as possible. 'Then, one – two – three!'

Down came the linstocks on the touchholes, and almost simultaneously the guns roared out; even with the inevitable variation in the amounts of powder in the touchholes there was not a second between the first and the last of the fifteen explosions. Bush, his foot on the cable, felt the ship heave with the recoil – double-shotting the guns had increased the effect. The smoke came eddying into the sweltering heat, but Bush had no attention to give to it. The cable moved under his foot with the heave of the ship. Surely it was moving along. It was! He had to shift the position of his foot. The clank of a newly-gained pawl on the windlass could be heard by everyone. Clank – clank. Someone in the smoke started to cheer and others took it up.

'Silence!' bellowed Hornblower.

Clank – clank – clank. Reluctant sounds; but the ship was moving. The cable was coming in slowly, like a mortally-wounded monster. If only they could keep her on the move! Clank - clank - clank. The interval between the sounds was growing shorter - even Bush had to admit that to himself. The cable was coming in faster - faster.

'Take charge here, Mr Hornblower,' said Bush, and sprang for the main deck. If the ship were free there would be urgent matters for the first lieutenant to attend to. The capstan pawls seemed almost to be playing a merry tune, so rapidly did they sound as the capstan turned.

Undoubtedly there was much to be attended to on deck. There were decisions which must be made at once. Bush touched his hat to Buckland.

'Any orders, sir?'

Buckland turned unhappy eyes on him.

'We've lost the flood,' he said.

This must be the highest moment of the tide; if they were to touch ground again, kedging off would not be so simple an operation.

'Yes, sir,' said Bush.

The decision could only lie with Buckland; no one else could share the responsibility. But it was terribly hard for a man to have to admit defeat in his very first command. Buckland looked as if for inspiration round the bay, where the red-and-gold flags of Spain flew above the banked-up powder smoke of the batteries – no inspiration could be found there.

'We can only get out with the land breeze,' said Buckland.

'Yes, sir.'

There was almost no longer for the land breeze to blow, either, thought Bush; Buckland knew it as well as he did. A shot from the fort on the hill struck into the main-chains at that moment, with a jarring crash and a shower of splinters. They heard the call for the fire party, and with that Buckland reached the bitter decision.

'Heave in on the spring cable,' he ordered. 'Get her round head to sea.'

'Aye aye, sir.'

Retreat – defeat; that was what that order meant. But defeat had to be faced; even with that order given there was much that had to be done to work the ship out of the imminent danger in which she lay. Bush turned to give the orders.

''Vast heaving at the capstan, there!'

The clanking ceased and the *Renown* rode free in the muddy, churned-up waters of the bay. To retreat she would have to turn tail, reverse herself in that confined space, and work her way out to sea. Fortunately the means were immediately available: by heaving in on the bow cable which had so far lain idle between hawsehole and anchor, the ship could be brought short round.

'Cast off the stern cable messenger!'

The orders came quickly and easily; it was a routine piece of seamanship, even though it had to be carried out under fire of red-hot shot. There were the boats still manned and afloat to drag the battered vessel out of harm's way if the precarious breeze should die away. Round came the *Renown*'s bows under the pull of the bow cable as the capstan set to work upon it. Even though the wind was dying away to a sweltering calm, movement was obvious. While the capstan was dragging the ship up to her anchor the necessity for keeping the ship on the move occurred to Bush. He touched his hat to Buckland again.

'Shall I warp her down the bay, sir?'

Buckland had been standing by the binnacle staring

vacantly at the fort, but Bush's question prodded him back into dealing with the situation.

'Yes,' said Buckland, and Bush turned away, happy to have something useful to do which he well knew how to do.

Another anchor had to be cockbilled at the port bow, another cable roused out. A hail to James, in command of the boats since Roberts' death, told him of the new evolution and called him under the bows for the anchor to be lowered down to the launch – the trickiest part of the whole business. Then the launch's crew bent to their oars and rowed ahead, their boat crank with the ponderous weight that she bore dangling aft and with the cable paying out astern. Yard by yard, to the monotonous turning of the capstan, the *Renown* crept up to her first anchor, and when that cable was straight up and down the flutter of a signal warned James, now far ahead in the launch, to drop the anchor his boat carried and return for the stream anchor which was about to be hauled up. The effort of the capstan had to be transferred from one cable to the other, while the two cutters were given lines by which they could contribute their tiny effort to the general result, towing the ponderous ship and giving her the smallest conceivable amount of motion which yet was valuable when it was a matter of such urgency to withdraw the ship out of range.

Down below Hornblower was at work dragging forward the guns he had previously dragged aft; the rumble and squeal of the trucks over the planking was audible through the ship over the monotonous clanking of the capstan. Overhead blazed the pitiless sun, softening the pitch in the seams, while yard after painful yard the ship crept on down the bay out of range of the red-hot shot, over the glittering still water; down the bay of Samaná until at last they were out of range, and could pause while the men drank a niggardly half-pint of warm odorous water before turning back to their labours. To bury the dead, to repair the damages, and to digest the realization of defeat.

Taken by Surprise

Having failed in his first attempt to destroy the privateers, Buckland's inclination was to leave them alone and to make for Jamaica, but he could not help remembering the court of inquiry which he would have to face. If he could arrive with a victory to his credit and the privateers as prizes, he would be welcomed and commended for his success, and the court would be much more ready to rule that he had acted rightly in placing Captain Sawyer under restraint than if he could only report a defeat in which nine men had been killed and twenty wounded. He therefore decided to send for Hornblower and hear his suggestions, which Bush had mentioned to him.

Hornblower proposed a speedy return to Scotchman's Bay, the landing by night of a hundred seamen and eighty marines, and a surprise attack on the fort at dawn. As usual Buckland hesitated: he saw the opportunity to redeem the failure of his first attempt and win a resounding success; he also saw the possibility of a second and far more disastrous defeat; but in the end he agreed and ordered Bush to assume command of the attacking force, with Hornblower second-in-command.

As soon as the plan was settled, the ship was set on her course for Scotchman's Bay, which lay on the other side of the long, narrow promontory on which the fort stood, and the organization of the landing party was begun without delay. Shortly before midnight they reached the sandy beach which Hornblower had spotted when the Renown was hove-to and wallowing off the coast two mornings previously, and which he had marked down in spite of his seasickness as the best place for making a landing.

125

THE sea breeze had died away with the cooling of the land, and it was that breathless time of night when air pressures over island and ocean were evenly balanced. Not many miles out at sea the trade winds could blow, as they blew eternally, but here on the beach a humid calm prevailed. The long swell of the Atlantic broke momentarily at the first hint of shallows far out, but lived on, like some once vigorous man now feeble after an illness, to burst rhythmically in foam on the beach to the westward; here, where the limestone cliffs of the Samaná peninsula began, there was a sheltered corner where a small watercourse had worn a wide gully in the cliff, at the most easterly end of the wide beach. And sea and surf and beach seemed to be afire; in the dark night the phosphorescence of the water was vividly bright, heaving up with the surf, running up the beach with the breakers, and lighting up the oar blades as the launches pulled to shore. The boats seemed to be floating on fire which derived new life from their passage; each launch left a wake of fire behind it, with a vivid streak on either side where the oar blades had bitten into the water.

Both landing and ascent were easy at the foot of the gully; the launches nuzzled their bows into the sand and the landing party had only to climb out, thigh-deep in the water – thigh-deep in liquid fire – holding their weapons and cartridge boxes high to make sure they were not wetted. Even the experienced seamen in the party were impressed by the brightness of the phosphorescence; the raw hands were excited by it enough to raise a bubbling chatter which called for a sharp order to repress it. Bush was one of the earliest to climb out of his launch; he splashed ashore and stood on the unaccustomed solidity of the beach while the others followed him; the water streamed down out of his soggy trouser legs.

A dark figure appeared before him, coming from the direction of the other launch.

'My party is all ashore, sir,' it reported.

'Very good, Mr Hornblower.'

'I'll start up the gully with the advanced guard then, sir?'

'Yes, Mr Hornblower. Carry out your orders.'

Bush was tense and excited, as far as his stoical training and phlegmatic temperament would allow him to be; he would have liked to plunge into action at once, but the careful scheme worked out in consultation with Hornblower did not allow it. He stood aside while his own party was being formed up and Hornblower called the other division to order.

'Starbowlines! Follow me closely. Every man is to keep in touch with the man ahead of him. Remember your muskets aren't loaded – it's no use snapping them if we meet an enemy. Cold steel for that. If any one of you is fool enough to load and fire he'll get four dozen at the gangway tomorrow. That I promise you. Woolton!'

'Sir!'

'Bring up the rear. Now follow me, you men, starting from the right of the line.'

Hornblower's party filed off into the darkness. Already the marines were coming ashore, their scarlet tunics black against the phosphorescence. The white crossbelts were faintly visible side by side in a rigid two-deep line as they formed up, the non-commissioned officers snapping low-voiced orders at them. With his left hand still resting on his sword-hilt, Bush checked once more with his right hand that his pistols were in his belt and his cartridges in his pocket. A shadowy figure halted before him with a military click of the heels.

'All present and correct, sir. Ready to march off,' said Captain Whiting, the senior marine officer.

'Thank you. We may as well start. Mr Abbot!'

'Sir!'

'You have your orders. I'm leaving with the marine detachment now. Follow us.'

'Aye aye, sir.'

It was a long, hard climb up the gully; the sand soon was replaced by rock, with steep ledges up which Bush had to heave himself. In a few minutes he was streaming with sweat, but he climbed on stubbornly. Behind him the marines followed clumsily, boots clashing, weapons and equipment clinking, so that anyone might think the noise would be heard a mile away. Someone slipped and swore.

'Keep a still tongue in yer 'ead!' snapped a corporal.

'Silence!' snarled Whiting over his shoulder.

Onward and upward; here and there the vegetation was lofty enough to cut off the faint light from the stars, and Bush had to grope his way along over the rock, his breath coming with difficulty, powerfully built man though he was. Fireflies showed here and there as he climbed; it was years since he had seen fireflies last, but he paid no attention to them now. They excited irrepressible comment among the marines following him, though; Bush felt a bitter rage against the uncontrolled louts who were imperilling everything – their own lives as well as the success of the expedition – by their silly comments.

'I'll deal with 'em, sir,' said Whiting, and dropped back to let the column overtake him.

Higher up a squeaky voice, moderated as best its owner knew how, greeted him from the darkness ahead.

'Mr Bush, sir?'

'Yes.'

'This is Wellard, sir. Mr Hornblower sent me back here to act as guide. There's grassland beginning just above here.'

'Very well,' said Bush.

He halted for a space, wiping his streaming face with his coat-sleeve, while the column closed up behind him. It was not much farther to climb when he moved on again; Wellard led him past a clump of shadowy trees, and, sure enough, Bush felt grass under his feet, and he could walk more freely, uphill still, but only a gentle slope compared with the gully. There was a low challenge ahead of them.

'Friend,' said Wellard. 'This is Mr Bush here.'

'Glad to see you, sir,' said another voice – Hornblower's.

Hornblower detached himself from the darkness and came forward to make his report.

'My party is formed up just ahead, sir. I've sent Saddler and two reliable men on as scouts.'

'Very good,' said Bush, and meant it.

The marine sergeant was reporting to Whiting.

'All present, sir, 'cept for Chapman, sir. 'E's sprained 'is ankle, or 'e says 'e 'as, sir. Left 'im be'ind back there, sir.'

'Let your men rest, Captain Whiting,' said Bush.

Life in the confines of a ship of the line was no sort of training for climbing cliffs in the tropics, especially as the day before had been exhausting.

'We're on the crest here, sir,' said Hornblower. 'You can see over into the bay from that side there.'

'Three miles from the fort, d'ye think?'

Bush did not mean to ask a question, for he was in

command, but Hornblower was so ready with his report that Bush could not help doing so.

'Perhaps. Less than four, anyway, sir. Dawn in four hours from now, and the moon rises in half an hour.'

'Yes.'

'There's some sort of track or path along the crest, sir, as you'd expect. It should lead to the fort.'

'Thank you, Mr Hornblower. We'll move forward. Start with your division, if you please.'

'Aye aye, sir.'

The advance began. The domed limestone top of the peninsula was covered with long grass, interspersed with occasional trees. Off the track walking was a little difficult on account of the toughness and irregularity of the bunches of high grass, but on the track it was comparatively easy. The men could move along it in something like a solid body, well closed up. Their eyes, thoroughly accustomed to the darkness, could see in the starlight enough to enable them to pick their way.

Bush plodded on at the head of the marines with Whiting at his side, the darkness all about him like a warm blanket. There was a kind of dreamlike quality about the march, induced perhaps by the fact that Bush had not slept for twenty-four hours and was stupid with the fatigues he had undergone during that period.

'Ah!' said Whiting suddenly.

The path had wandered to the right, away from the sea and towards the bay, and now they had crossed the backbone of the peninsula and opened up the view over the bay. On their right they could see clear down the bay to the sea, and there it was not quite dark, for above the horizon a little moonlight was struggling through the clouds that lay at the lower edge of the sky.

'Mr Bush, sir?'

This was Wellard, his voice more under command this time.

'Here I am.'

'Mr Hornblower sent me back again, sir. We've come across some cattle, sir. Asleep on the hill. We disturbed 'em and they're wandering about.'

'Thank you, I understand,' said Bush.

Bush had the lowest opinion of the ordinary man and the sub-ordinary man who constituted the great bulk of his command. He knew perfectly well that if they were to blunder into cattle along this path they would think they were meeting the enemy. There would be excitement and noise, even if there was no shooting.

'Tell Mr Hornblower I am going to halt for fifteen minutes.'

'Aye aye, sir.'

A rest and opportunity to close up the column were desirable for the weary men in any case, as long as there was time to spare. And during the rest the men could be personally and individually warned about the possibility of encountering cattle. Bush knew that merely to pass the word back down the column would be unsatisfactory, actually unsafe, with these tired and slow-witted men.

When the column moved forward again Hornblower's unmistakable gangling figure showed up ahead, silhouetted against the faint moonlight. He fell into step beside Bush and made his report.

'I've sighted the fort, sir.'

'You have?'

'Yes, sir. A mile ahead from here, or thereabouts, there's a gully. The fort's beyond that. You can see it against the moon. Maybe half a mile beyond, maybe less. I've left Wellard and Saddler at the gully with orders to halt the advance there.'

'Thank you.'

Bush plodded on over the uneven surface. Now despite his fatigue he was growing tense again, as the tiger having scented his prey braces his muscles for the spring. Bush was a fighting man, and the thought of action close ahead acted as a stimulant to him. Two hours to sunrise; time and to spare.

'Half a mile from the gully to the fort?' he asked.

'Less than that, I should say, sir.'

'Very well. I'll halt there and wait for daylight.'

'Yes, sir. May I go on to join my division?'

'You may, Mr Hornblower.'

Bush and Whiting were holding down the pace of the march to a slow methodical step, adapted to the capacity of the slowest and clumsiest man in the column; Bush at this moment was checking himself from lengthening his stride under the spur of the prospect of action. Hornblower went plunging ahead; Bush could see his awkward gait, but found himself approving of his subordinate's overflowing energy. He began to discuss with Whiting plans for the final assault.

There was a petty officer waiting for them at the approach to the gully. Bush passed the word back for the column to be ready to halt, and then halted it. He went forward to reconnoitre; with Whiting and Hornblower beside him he stared forward at the square silhouette of the fort against the sky. It even seemed possible to see the dark line of the flagpole. Now his tenseness was eased; the scowl that had been on his face in the last stages of the advance had softened into an expression of good humour, which was wasted in the circumstances.

The arrangements were quickly made, the orders whispered back and forth, the final warnings given. It was the most dangerous moment so far, as the men had to be moved up into the gully and deployed ready for a rush. One whisper from Whiting called for more than a moment's cogitation from Bush.

'Shall I give permission for the men to load, sir?'

'No,' answered Bush at length. 'Cold steel.'

It would be too much of a risk to allow all those muskets to be loaded in the dark. There would not only be the noise of the ramrods, but there was also the danger of some fool pulling a trigger. Hornblower went off to the left, Whiting with his marines to the right, and Bush lay down in the midst of his division in the centre. His legs ached with their unaccustomed exercise, and as he lay his head was inclined to swim with fatigue and lack of sleep. He roused himself and sat up so as to bring himself under control again. Except for his weariness he did not find the waiting period troublesome to him; years of life at sea with its uncounted eventless watches, and years of war with its endless periods of boredom, had inured him to waiting. Some of the seamen actually slept as they lay in the rocky gully; more than once Bush heard snores begin, abruptly cut off by the nudges of the snorers' neighbours.

Now there, at last, right ahead, beyond the fort – was the sky a little paler? Or was it merely that the moon had climbed above the cloud? All round about save there the sky was like purple velvet, still spangled with stars. But there – there – undoubtedly there was a pallor in the sky which had not been there before. Bush stirred and felt again at the uncomfortable pistols in his belt. They were at half-cock; he must remember to pull the hammers back. On the horizon there was a suspicion, the merest suggestion, of a redness mingled with the purple of the sky.

'Pass the word down the line,' said Bush. 'Prepare to attack.'

He waited for the word to pass, but in less time than was possible for it to have reached the ends of the line there were sounds and disturbances in the gully. The damned fools who were always to be found in any body of men had started to rise as soon as the word had reached them, probably without even bothering to pass the word on themselves. But the example would be infectious, at least; beginning at the wings, and coming back to the centre where Bush was, a double ripple of men rising to their feet went along the line. Bush rose too. He drew his sword, balanced it in his hand, and when he was satisfied with his grip he drew a pistol with his left hand and pulled back the hammer. Over on the right there was a sudden clatter of metal; the marines were fixing their bayonets. Bush could see the faces now of the men to right and to left of him.

'Forward!' he said, and the line came surging up out of the gully. 'Steady, there!'

He said the last words almost loudly; sooner or later the hotheads in the line would start to run, and later would be better than sooner. He wanted his men to reach the fort in a single wave, not in a succession of breathless individuals. Out on the left he heard Hornblower's voice saying 'Steady' as well. The noise of the advance must reach the fort now, must attract the attention even of sleepy, careless Spanish sentries. Soon a sentry would call for his sergeant, the sergeant would come to see, would hesitate a moment, and then give the alarm. The fort bulked square in front of Bush, still shadowy black against the newly red sky; he simply could not restrain himself from quickening his step, and the line came hurrying forward along with him. Then someone raised

*'Forward!' he said, and the line came surging up out
of the gully*

a shout, and then the other hotheads shouted, and the whole line started to run, Bush running with them.

Like magic, they were at the edge of the ditch, a six-foot scarp, almost vertical, cut in the limestone.

'Come on!' shouted Bush.

Even with his sword and his pistol in his hands he was able to precipitate himself down the scarp, turning his back to the fort and clinging to the edge with his elbows before allowing himself to drop. The bottom of the dry ditch was slippery and irregular, but he plunged across it to the opposite scarp. Yelling men clustered along it, hauling themselves up.

'Give me a hoist!' shouted Bush to the men on either side of him, and they put their shoulders to his thighs and almost threw him up bodily. He found himself on his face, lying on the narrow shelf above the ditch at the foot of the ramparts. A few yards along a seaman was already trying to fling his grapnel up to the top. It came thundering down, missing Bush by no more than a yard, but the seaman, without a glance at him, snatched it back, poised himself again and flung the grapnel up the ramparts. It caught, and the seaman, setting his feet against the ramparts and grasping the line with his hands, began to climb like a madman. Before he was halfway up another seaman had grabbed the line and started to scale the ramparts after him, and a yelling crowd of excited men gathered round contending for the next place. Farther along the foot of the ramparts another grapnel had caught and another crowd of yelling men were gathered about the line. Now there was musketry fire; a good many loud reports, and a whiff of powder smoke came to Bush's nostrils in sharp contrast with the pure night air that he had been breathing.

Round on the other face of the fort on his right the

marines would be trying to burst in through the embrasures of the guns; Bush turned to his left to see what could be done there. Almost instantly he found his reward; here was the sally port into the fort – a wide wooden door bound with iron, sheltered in the angle of the small projecting bastion at the corner of the fort. Bush raised his voice so that it pealed like a trumpet above the din.

'Axemen here! Axemen! Axemen!'

There were still plenty of men down in the ditch who had not yet had time to scale the scarp; one of them, waving an axe, plunged through the crowd and began to climb up. But Silk, the immensely powerful bosun's mate who commanded a section of seamen in Bush's division, came running along the shelf and grabbed the axe. He began to hew at the door, with tremendous methodical blows, gathering his body together and then flinging the axehead into the wood with all the strength in his body. Another axeman arrived, elbowed Bush aside, and started to hack at the door as well, but he was neither as acccomplished nor as powerful. The thunder of their blows resounded in the angle. The iron-barred wicket in the door opened, with a gleam of steel beyond the bars. Bush pointed his pistol and fired. Silk's axe drove clean through the door, and he wrenched the blade free; then, changing his aim, he began to swing the axe in a horizontal arc at the middle part of the door. Three mighty blows and he paused to direct the other axeman where to strike. Silk struck again and again; then he put down the axe, set his fingers in the jagged hole that had opened, his foot against the door, and with one frightful, muscle-tearing effort he rent away a whole section of the door. There was a beam across the gap he had opened; Silk's axe crashed on to it and through it, and again.

With a hoarse shout Silk plunged, axe in hand, through the jagged hole.

'Come along, men!' yelled Bush, at the top of his lungs, and plunged through after him.

This was the open courtyard of the fort. Bush stumbled over a dead man and looked up to see a group of men before him, in their shirts, or naked; coffee-coloured faces with long, disordered moustaches; men with cutlasses and pistols. Silk flung himself upon them like a maniac, the axe swinging. A Spaniard fell under the axe; Bush saw a severed finger fall to the ground as the axe crashed through the Spaniard's ineffectual guard. Pistols banged and smoke eddied about as Bush rushed forward too. There were other men swarming after him. Bush's sword clashed against a cutlass and then the group turned and fled. Bush swung with his sword at a naked shoulder fleeing before him, and saw a red wound open in the flesh and heard the man scream. The man he was pursuing vanished somewhere, like a wraith, and Bush, hurrying on to find other enemies, met a red-coated marine, hatless, his hair wild and his eyes blazing, yelling like a fiend. Bush actually had to parry the bayonet-thrust the marine made at him.

'Steady, you fool!' shouted Bush, only conscious after the words had passed his lips that they were spoken at the top of his voice.

There was a hint of recognition in the marine's mad eyes, and he turned aside, his bayonet at the charge, and rushed on. There were other marines in the background; they must have made their way in through the embrasures. They were all yelling, all drunk with fighting. And here was another rush of seamen, swarming down from the ramparts they had scaled. On the far side there were wooden buildings; his men were swarming round them and shots and screams were echoing from them. Those must be the barracks and storehouses, and the garrison must have fled there for shelter from the fury of the stormers.

Whiting appeared, his scarlet tunic filthy, his sword dangling from his wrist. His eyes were bleary and cloudy.

'Call 'em off,' said Bush, grasping at his own sanity with a desperate effort.

It took Whiting a moment to recognize him and to understand the order.

'Yes, sir,' he said.

A fresh flood of seamen came pouring into view beyond the buildings; Hornblower's division had found its way into the fort on the far side, evidently. Bush looked round him and called to a group of his own men who appeared at that moment.

'Follow me,' he said, and pushed on.

A ramp with an easy slope led up the side of the ramparts. A dead man lay there, half-way up, but Bush gave the corpse no more attention than it deserved. At the top was the main battery, six huge guns pointing through the embrasures. And beyond was the sky, all bloody-red with the dawn. A third of the way up to the zenith reached the significant colour, but even while Bush halted to look at it a golden gleam of sun showed through the clouds on the horizon, and the red began to fade perceptibly; blue sky and white clouds and blazing golden sun took its place. That was the measure of the time the assault had taken; only the few minutes from earliest dawn to tropical sunrise. Bush stood and grasped this astonishing fact – it could have been late afternoon as far as his own sensations went.

Here from the gun platform the whole view of the bay opened up. There was the opposite shore; the shallows where the *Renown* had grounded (was it only yesterday?), the rolling country lifting immediately into the hills of that side, with the sharply defined shape of the other battery at the foot of the point. To the left the peninsula dropped sharply in a series of jagged headlands, stretching like fingers out into the blue, blue ocean; farther round still was the sapphire surface of Scotchman's Bay, and there, with her backed mizen topsail catching brilliantly the rising sun, lay the *Renown*. At that distance she looked like a lovely toy; Bush caught his breath at the sight of her, not because of the beauty of the scene, but with relief. The sight of the ship, and the associated memories which the sight called up in his mind, brought his sanity flooding back; there were a thousand things to be done now.

Hornblower appeared up the other ramp; he looked like a scarecrow with his disordered clothes. He held sword in one hand and pistol in the other, just as did Bush. Beside him Wellard swung a cutlass singularly large for him, and at his heels were a score or more of seamen still under discipline, their muskets, with bayonets fixed, held before them ready for action.

'Morning, sir,' said Hornblower. His battered cocked hat was still on his head for him to touch it, and he made a move to do so, checking himself at the realization that his sword was in his hand.

'Good morning,' said Bush, automatically.

'Congratulations, sir,' said Hornblower. His face was white, and the smile on his lips was like the grin of a corpse. His beard sprouted over his lips and chin.

'Thank you,' said Bush.

Hornblower pushed his pistol into his belt and then sheathed his sword.

'I've taken possession of all that side, sir,' he went on, with a gesture behind him. 'Shall I carry on?'

'Yes, carry on, Mr Hornblower.'

'Aye aye, sir.'

This time Hornblower could touch his hat. He gave a rapid order posting a petty officer and men over the guns.

'You see, sir,' said Hornblower, pointing, 'a few got away.'

Bush looked down the precipitous hillside that fell to the bay and could see a few figures down there.

'Not enough to trouble us,' he said; his mind was just beginning to work smoothly now.

'No, sir. I've forty prisoners under guard at the main gate. I can see Whiting's collecting the rest. I'll go on now, sir, if I may.'

'Very well, Mr Hornblower.'

Somebody at least had kept a clear head during the fury of the assault. Bush went on down the farther ramp. A petty officer and a couple of seamen stood there on guard; they came to attention as Bush appeared.

'What are you doing?' he asked.

'This yere's the magazine, zur,' said the petty officer – Ambrose, captain of the foretop, who had never lost the broad Devon acquired in his childhood, despite his years in the navy. 'We'm guarding of it.'

'Mr Hornblower's orders?'

'Iss, zur.'

A forlorn party of prisoners were squatting by the main gate. Hornblower had reported the presence of them. But there were guards he had said nothing about: a sentry at the well; guards at the gate; Woolton, the steadiest petty officer of them all, at a long wooden building beside the gate, and six men with him.

'What's your duty?' demanded Bush.

'Guarding the provision store, sir. There's liquor here.'

'Very well.'

If the madmen who had made the assault – that marine, for instance, whose bayonet-thrust Bush had parried – had got at the liquor there would be no controlling them at all.

Abbott, the midshipman in subordinate command of Bush's own division, came hurrying up.

'What the hell d'ye think you've been doing?' demanded Bush, testily. 'I've been without you since the attack began.'

'Sorry, sir,' apologized Abbott. Of course he had been carried away by the fury of the attack, but that was no excuse; certainly no excuse when one remembered young Wellard still at Hornblower's side and attending to his duties.

'Get ready to make the signal to the ship,' ordered Bush. 'You ought to have been ready to do that five minutes ago. Clear three guns. Who was it who was carrying the flag? Find him and bend it on over the Spanish colours. Jump to it, damn you.'

Victory might be sweet, but it had no effect on Bush's temper, now that the reaction had set in. Bush had had no sleep and no breakfast, and even though perhaps only ten minutes had elapsed since the fort had been captured, his conscience nagged at him regarding those ten minutes; there were many things he ought to have done in that time.

It was a relief to turn away from the contemplation of his own shortcomings and to settle with Whiting regarding the safeguarding of the prisoners. They had all been fetched out of the barrack buildings by now; a hundred half-naked men, and at least a score of women, their hair streaming down their backs and their scanty clothing clutched about them. Among the men there was a small sprinkling of Negroes and mulattoes, but most of them were Spaniards. Nearly all the dead men who lay here and there were fully clothed, in white uniforms with blue facings – they were the sentinels and the main guard who had paid the penalty for their lack of watchfulness.

'Who was in command?' asked Bush of Whiting.

'Can't tell, sir.'

'Well, ask them, then.'

Bush had command of no language at all save his own, and apparently neither had Whiting, judging by his unhappy glance.

'Please, sir – ' This was Pierce, surgeon's mate, trying to attract his attention. 'Can I have a party to help carry the wounded into the shade?'

Before Bush could answer him Abbott was hailing from the gun platform.

'Guns clear, sir. May I draw powder charges from the magazines?'

And then, before Bush could give permission, here was young Wellard, trying to elbow Pierce on one side so as to command Bush's attention.

'Please, sir. Please, sir. Mr Hornblower's respects, sir, an' could you please come up to the tower there, sir. Mr Hornblower says it's urgent, sir.'

Bush felt at that moment as if one more distraction would break his heart.

Red-Hot Shot

A T each corner of the fort there was a small bastion
built out, to give flanking fire along the walls, and
on top of the south-west bastion stood a little
watch-tower which carried the flagstaff. Bush and Hornblower stood on the tower, the broad Atlantic behind
them and before them the long gulf of the bay of Samaná.
Over their heads waved two flags; the White Ensign
above, the red and gold of Spain below. Out in the
Renown they might not be able to make out the colours,
but they would certainly see the two flags. And when,
having heard the three signal guns boom out, they trained
their telescopes on the fort, they must have seen the flags
slowly flutter down and rise again, dip and rise again.
Three guns; two flags twice dipped. That was the signal
that the fort was in English hands, and the *Renown* had
seen it, for she had braced up her mizen topsail and
begun the long beat back along the coast of the peninsula.

Bush and Hornblower had with them the one telescope
which a hasty search through the fort had brought to
light; when one of them had it to his eye the other could
hardly restrain his twitching fingers from snatching at it.
At the moment Bush was looking through it, training it
on the farther shore of the bay, and Hornblower was
stabbing with an index finger at what he had been looking
at a moment before.

'You see, sir?' he asked. 'Farther up the bay than the
battery. There's the town – Savana, it's called. And
beyond that there's the shipping. They'll up anchor any
minute now.'

'I see 'em,' said Bush, the glass still at his eye. 'Four small craft. No sail hoisted – hard to tell what they are.'

'Easy enough to guess, though, sir.'

'Yes, I suppose so,' said Bush.

There would be no need for big men-of-war here, immediately adjacent to the Mona Passage. Half the Caribbean trade came up through here, passing within thirty miles of the bay of Samaná. Fast, handy craft, with a couple of long guns each and a large crew, could dash out and snap up prizes and retire to the protection of the bay, where the crossed fire of the batteries could be relied on to keep out enemies, as the events of yesterday had proved. The raiders would hardly have to spend a night at sea.

'They'll know by now we've got this fort,' said Hornblower. 'They'll guess that *Renown* will be coming round after 'em. They can sweep, and tow, and kedge. They'll be out of the bay before you can say Jack Robinson. And from Engano Point it's a fair wind for Martinique.'

'Very likely,' agreed Bush.

With a simultaneous thought they turned to look at the *Renown*. With her stern to them, her sails braced sharp on the starboard tack, she was making her way out to sea; it would be a long beat before she could go about in the certainty of being able to weather Cape Samaná. She looked lovely enough out there, with her white sails against the rich blue, but it would be hours before she could work round to stop the bolt-hole. Bush turned back and considered the sheltered waters of the bay.

'Better man the guns and make ready for 'em,' he said.

'Yes, sir,' said Hornblower. He hesitated. 'We won't have 'em under fire for long. They'll be shallow draught.

They can hug the point over there closer than *Renown* could.'

'But it won't take much to sink 'em, either,' said Bush. 'Oh, I see what you're after.'

'Red-hot shot might make all the difference, sir,' said Hornblower.

'Repay 'em in their own coin,' said Bush, with a grin of satisfaction. Yesterday the *Renown* had endured the hellish fire of red-hot shot. To Bush, the thought of roasting a few Dagoes was quite charming.

'That's right, sir,' said Hornblower.

He was not grinning like Bush. There was a frown on his face; he was oppressed with the thought that the privateers might escape to continue their depredations elsewhere, and any means to reduce their chances should be used.

'But can you do it?' asked Bush suddenly. 'D'ye know how to heat shot?'

'I'll find out, sir.'

'I'll wager no man of ours knows how.'

Shot could only be heated in a battery on land; a sea-going ship, constructed of inflammable material, could not run the risk of going into action with a flaming furnace inside her. Sea-going men left the use of the heated weapon to shore-based garrison artillery.

'I'll try and find out for myself, sir,' said Hornblower. 'There's the furnace down there and all the gear.'

Hornblower stood in the sunshine, already far too hot to be comfortable. His face was pale, dirty and bearded and in his expression eagerness and weariness were oddly at war. Bush found the telescope leaving his hand and passing into Hornblower's.

'May I have another look, sir, before I go down? By George, I thought as much. That two-master's warping

out, sir. Less than an hour before she's within range.
I'll get the guns manned, sir. Take a look for yourself,
sir.'

He went darting down the stone stairs of the tower.
Bush's glance through the telescope confirmed what
Hornblower had said. At least one of the vessels up the
bay was beginning to move. He turned and swept the
rest of the land and water with a precautionary glance
before handing the telescope to Abbott, who during all
this conversation had been standing by, silent in the
presence of his betters.

'Keep a sharp look-out,' said Bush.

Down in the body of the fort Hornblower was already
issuing rapid orders, and the men, roused to activity,
were on the move. On the gun platform they were casting
loose the remaining guns, and as Bush descended from
the platform he saw Hornblower organizing other working
parties, snapping out orders with quick gestures. There
was the usual group of people clamouring for Bush's
attention, for orders and information, and by the time he
had dealt with them there was smoke rising from the
furnace in the corner of the courtyard, and a loud crack-
ling from inside it. Bush walked over. A seaman, kneeling,
was plying a pair of bellows; two other men were bringing
wood from the pile against the ramparts. When the
furnace door was opened the blast of heat that rose into
Bush's face was enough to make him step back. Hornblower turned up with his hurried pace.

'How's the shot, Saddler?' he asked.

The petty officer picked up some rags, and, with them
to shield his hands, laid hold of two long handles that
projected from the far side of the furnace, balancing
two projecting from the near side. When he drew them
out it became apparent that all four handles were part

of a large iron grating, the centre of which rested inside the furnace above the blazing fuel. Lying on the grating were rows of shot, still black in the sunshine. Saddler shifted his quid, gathered his saliva, and spat expertly on the nearest one. The spittle boiled off, but not with violence.

'Not very hot yet, sir,' said Saddler.

'Us'll fry they devils,' said the man with the bellows, unexpectedly; he looked up, as he crouched on his knees, with ecstasy in his face at the thought of burning his enemies alive.

Hornblower paid him no attention.

'Here, you bearer men,' he said, 'let's see what you can do.'

Hornblower had been followed by a file of men, every pair carrying a piece of apparatus formed of two iron bars joined with iron crosspieces. The first pair approached. Saddler took a pair of tongs and gingerly worked a hot shot on to the bearer.

'Move on, you two,' ordered Hornblower. 'Next!'

When a shot lay on every bearer Hornblower led his men away.

'Now let's see you roll those into the guns,' he said.

Bush followed, consumed with curiosity. The procession moved up the ramp to the gun platform, where now crews had been told off to every gun; the guns were run back with the muzzles well clear of the embrasures. Tubs of water stood by each pair of guns.

'Now, you rammers,' said Hornblower, 'are your dry wads in? Then in with your wet wads.'

From the tubs the seamen brought out round, flat discs of fibre, dripping with water.

'Two to a gun,' said Hornblower.

The wet wads were thrust into the muzzles of the guns

and then were forced down the bores with the club-ended ramrods.

'Ram 'em home,' said Hornblower. 'Now, bearers.'

It was not such an easy thing to do, to put the ends of the bearing-stretchers at the muzzles of the guns and then to tilt so as to induce the hot shot to roll down into the bore.

'The Don must've exercised with these guns better than we'd give 'em credit for,' said Hornblower to Bush, 'judging by the practice they made yesterday. Rammers!'

The ramrods thrust the shot home against the charges; there was a sharp sizzling noise as each hot shot rested against the wet wads.

'Run up!'

The guns' crews seized the tackles and heaved, and the ponderous guns rolled slowly forward to point their muzzles out through the embrasures.

'Aim for the point over there and fire!'

With handspikes under the rear axles the guns were traversed at the orders of the captains; the priming tubes were already in the touchholes and each gun was fired as it bore. The sound of the explosions was very different here on the stone platform from when guns were fired in the confined spaces of a wooden ship. The slight wind blew the smoke sideways.

'Pretty fair!' said Hornblower, shading his eyes to watch the fall of the shot; and, turning to Bush, 'That'll puzzle those gentlemen over there. They'll wonder what in the world we're firing at.'

'How long,' asked Bush, who had watched the whole process with a fascinated yet horrified interest, 'before a hot shot burns through those wads and sets off the gun itself?'

'That is one of the things I do not know, sir,' answered

Hornblower with a grin. 'It would not surprise me if we found out during the course of today.'

'I dare say,' said Bush; but Hornblower had swung round and was confronting a seaman who had come running up to the platform.

'What d'ye think you're doing?'

'Bringing a fresh charge, sir,' said the man, surprised, indicating with a gesture the cartridge-container he carried.

'Then get back and wait for the order. Get back, all of you.'

The ammunition carriers shrank back before his evident anger.

'Swab out!' ordered Hornblower to the guns' crews, and as the wetted sponges were thrust into the muzzles he turned to Bush again. 'We can't be too careful, sir. We don't want any chance of live charges and red-hot shot coming together on this platform.'

'Certainly not,' agreed Bush.

He was both pleased and irritated that Hornblower should have dealt so efficiently with the organization of the battery.

'Fresh charges!' yelled Hornblower, and the ammunition carriers he had previously sent back came trotting up the ramp again. 'These are English cartridges, sir, I'll wager.'

'Why do you say that?'

'West Country serge, stitched and choked exactly like ours, sir. Out of English prizes, I fancy.'

Bush strained his sight to look at the four vessels creeping down the fairway. As he watched he saw the first one hoisting sail on both masts. Apparently she was taking advantage of a flaw of wind, blowing flukily in the confined and heated waters, to gain some of the desperately necessary distance towards the sea and safety.

'Mr Abbott, bring down that glass!' shouted Hornblower.

Through the telescope details were far plainer. Two large schooners with several guns a-side; a big lugger, and a vessel whose rig they still could not determine, as she was the farthest away and, with no sail set, was towing behind her boats out from the anchorage.

'It'll be long range, Mr Hornblower,' said Bush.

'Yes, sir. But they hit us with these same guns yesterday.'

Now the leading schooner had taken in her sail again; the wind here, what there was of it, was foul for her when she turned to port along the channel. She had two boats out quickly enough to tow her; Bush's telescope could reveal every detail.

'Some time yet before she's in range, sir,' said Hornblower. 'I'll take a look at the furnace, with your permission.'

'I'll come, too,' said Bush.

At the furnace the bellows were still being worked and the heat was tremendous – but it was far hotter when Saddler drew out the grating that carried the heated shot. Even in the sunshine they could see the glow of the spheres; as the heat rose from them the atmosphere above them wavered so that everything was vague and distorted. It could be a scene in Hell. Saddler spat on the nearest cannon ball and the saliva leaped with an instant hiss from the smooth surface of the sphere, falling from it without contact to dance and leap on the grating under it until with a final hiss it vanished entirely. A second attempt by Saddler brought the same result.

'Hot enough, sir?' asked Saddler.

'Yes,' said Hornblower.

Saddler thrust the grating back into the furnace and wiped his streaming face with the rags that had shielded his hands.

'Stand by, you bearer men,' said Hornblower. 'You'll be busy enough soon.'

With a glance at Bush for permission he was off again, back to the battery, hurrying with awkward, galvanic strides. Bush followed more slowly; he was weary with all his exertions, and it crossed his mind as he watched Hornblower hurrying up the ramp that Hornblower had probably been more active than he and was not blessed with nearly as powerful a physique. By the time he came up to him Hornblower was watching the leading schooner again.

'She's setting sail again!' said Bush. 'They've got her head round.'

'And the tows have cast off,' added Hornblower. 'Not long now.'

He looked down the line of guns, all charged and primed, the quoins withdrawn so that they were at their highest elevation, the muzzles pointing upward as though awaiting the shot to be rolled into them. The schooner was moving perceptibly down the channel towards them. Hornblower turned and walked down the row; behind his back one hand was twisting impatiently within the other; he came back and turned again, walking jerkily down the row – he seemed incapable of standing still, but when he caught Bush's eye on him he halted guiltily, forcing himself, with an obvious effort, to stand still like his superior officer. The schooner crept on, a full half-mile ahead of the next vessel.

'You might try a ranging shot,' said Bush at length.

'Aye aye, sir,' said Hornblower with instant agreement,

like a river bursting through a broken dam. It seemed as if he had been compelling himself to wait until Bush should speak.

'Furnace, there!' hailed Hornblower. 'Saddler! Send up one shot.'

The bearers came plodding up the ramp, carrying carefully between them the glowing cannon ball. The bright redness of it was quite obvious – even the heat that it gave off was distinctly perceptible. The wet wads were rammed down the bore of the nearest gun, the shot-bearer was hoisted up level with its muzzle, and, coaxed into motion with wad-hook and rammer, the fiery shot was rolled in. There was an instant hissing and spluttering of steam as the ball came into contact with the wet wads; Bush wondered again how long it would be before the wads were burned through and the charge set off; the recoil would make it decidedly uncomfortable for anyone who happened to be aiming the gun at that moment.

'Run up!' Hornblower was giving the orders. The gun's crew heaved at the tackles and the gun rumbled forward.

Hornblower took his place behind the gun and, squatting down, he squinted along it.

'Trail right!' Tackles and handspikes heaved the gun around. 'A touch more! Steady! No, a touch left. Steady!'

Somewhat to Bush's relief Hornblower straightened himself and came from behind the gun. He leaped on to the parapet with his usual uncontrollable vigour and shaded his eyes; Bush at one side kept his telescope trained on the schooner.

'Fire!' said Hornblower.

The momentary hiss of the priming was drowned in the instant bellow of the gun. Bush saw the black line of the

'Fire!' said Hornblower

shot's path across the blue of the sky, reaching upward during the time it might take to draw a breath, sinking downward again; a strange sort of line, an inch long if he had to say its length, constantly renewing itself in front and constantly disappearing at its back end, and pointing straight at the schooner. It was still pointing at her, just above her – to that extent did the speed of the shot out-pace the recording of retina and brain – when Bush saw the splash, right in line with the schooner's bows. He took his eye from the telescope as the splash disappeared, to find Hornblower looking at him.

'A cable's length short,' he said, and Hornblower nodded agreement.

'We can open fire then, sir?' asked Hornblower.

'Yes, carry on, Mr Hornblower.'

The words were hardly out of his mouth before Hornblower was hailing again.

'Furnace, there! Five more shot!'

It took Bush a moment or two to see the point of that order. But clearly it was inadvisable to have hot shot and powder charges brought up on the platform at the same time; the gun that had been fired would have to remain unloaded until the other five had fired as well.

'All your wet wads in?' demanded Hornblower of the guns' crews. 'Certain? Carry on, then.'

The shot were coaxed into the muzzles of the guns; they hissed and spluttered against the wads.

'Run up. Now take your aim. Make sure of it, captains.'

The hissing and spluttering continued as the guns were trained.

'Fire when your gun bears!'

Hornblower was up on the parapet again; Bush could see perfectly well through the embrasure of the idle gun. The five guns all fired within a second or two of each other; through Bush's telescope the sky was streaked by the passage of their shot.

'Sponge out!' said Hornblower; and then, louder, 'Six charges!'

He came down to Bush.

'One splash pretty close,' said Bush.

'Two very short,' said Hornblower, 'and one far out on the right. I know who fired that one and I'll deal with him.'

'One splash I didn't see,' said Bush.

'Nor did I, sir. Clean over, perhaps. But possibly a hit.'

The men with the charges came running up to the platform, and the eager crews seized them and rammed them home and the dry wads on top of the charges.

'Six shot!' shouted Hornblower to Saddler; and then, to the gun captains, 'Prime. Put in your wet wads.'

'She's altered course,' said Bush. 'The range can't have changed much.'

'No, sir. Load and run up! Excuse me, sir.'

He went hurrying off to take his stand by the left-hand gun, which presumably was the one which had been incorrectly laid previously.

'Take your aim carefully,' he called from his new position. 'Fire when you're sure.'

Bush saw him squat behind the left-hand gun, but he himself applied his attention to observing the results of the shooting.

The cycle repeated itself; the guns roared, the men came running with fresh charges, the red-hot shot were brought up. The guns were fired again before Hornblower came back to Bush's side.

'You're hitting, I think,' said Bush. He turned back to look again through his glass. 'I think – by God, yes! Smoke! Smoke!'

A faint black cloud was just visible between the

schooner's masts. It thinned again, and Bush could not be perfectly sure. The nearest gun bellowed out, and a chance flaw of wind blew the powder smoke about them as they stood together, blotting out their view of the schooner.

'Confound it all!' said Bush, moving about restlessly in search of a better viewpoint.

The other guns went off almost simultaneously and added to the smoke.

'Bring up fresh charges!' yelled Hornblower, with the smoke eddying round him. 'See that you swab those guns out properly.'

The smoke eddied away, revealing the schooner, apparently unharmed, still creeping along the bay.

'The range is shortening and the guns are hot now,' said Hornblower; and then, louder, 'Gun captains! Get your quoins in!'

He hurried off to supervise the adjustment of the guns' elevation, and it was some seconds before he hailed again for hot shot to be brought up. In that time Bush noticed that the schooner's boats, which had been pulling in company with the schooner, were turning to run alongside her. That could mean that the schooner's captain was now sure that the flaws of wind would be sufficient to carry her round the point and safely to the mouth of the bay. The guns went off again in an irregular salvo, and Bush saw a trio of splashes rise from the water's surface close on the near side of the schooner.

'Fresh charges!' yelled Hornblower.

Bush saw the schooner swing round, presenting her stern to the battery and heading straight for the shallows of the farther shore. Then he saw a sudden fountain of black smoke appear spouting from the schooners' deck, and while this sight was rejoicing him he saw the schooner's

booms swing over as she took the ground. She was afire
and had been deliberately run ashore. The smoke was
dense about her hull, and while he held her in his telescope he saw her big white mainsail above the smoke
suddenly disintegrate and disappear – the flames had
caught it and whisked it away into nothing. He took the
telescope from his eye and looked round for Hornblower,
who was standing on the parapet again. Powder and
smoke had grimed his face, already dark with the growth
of his beard, and his teeth showed strangely white as he
grinned. The gunners were cheering, and the cheering
was being echoed by the rest of the landing party in the
fort.

A great jet of smoke came from the burning wreck,
reaching up and up from between her masts; the mainmast fell as they watched, and as it fell the report of the
explosion came to their ears across the water; the fire had
reached the schooner's powder store, and when the
smoke cleared a little they could see that she now lay on
the shore in two halves, blown asunder in the middle.
The foremast still stood for a moment on the forward
half, but it fell as they watched it; bows and stern were
blazing fiercely, while the boats with the crew rowed
away across the shallows.

'A nasty sight,' said Hornblower.

But Bush could see nothing unpleasant about the sight
of an enemy burning.

'Here comes the next,' he said. 'She must be nearly in
range.'

The second schooner, also with her boats in attendance,
was coming down the channel, her sails set. Hornblower
turned back to the guns.

'D'you see the next ship to aim at?' he called; and
received a fierce roar of agreement, before he turned

round to hail Saddler. 'Bring up those shot, bearer men.'

The procession of bearers with the glowing shot came up the ramp again – rightfully hot shot; the heat as each one went by – twenty-four pounds of white-hot iron – was like the passage of a wave. The routine of rolling the fiendish things into the gun muzzles proceeded. There were some loud remarks from the men at the guns, and one of the shot fell with a thump on the stone floor of the battery, and lay there glowing. Two other guns were still not loaded.

'What's wrong there?' demanded Hornblower.

'Please, sir – '

Hornblower was already striding over to see for himself. From the muzzle of one of the three loaded guns there was a curl of steam; in all three there was a wild hissing as the hot shot rested on the wet wads.

'Run up, train, and fire,' ordered Hornblower. 'Now what's the matter with you others? Roll that thing out of the way.'

'Shot won't fit, sir,' said more than one voice as someone with a wad-hook awkwardly rolled the fallen shot up against the parapet. The bearers of the other two stood by, sweating. Anything Hornblower could say in reply was drowned for the moment by the roar of one of the guns – the men were still at the tackles, and the gun had gone off on its own volition as they ran it up. A man sat crying out with pain, for the carriage had recoiled over his foot and blood was already pouring from it on to the stone floor. The captains of the other two loaded guns made no pretence at training and aiming. The moment their guns were run up they shouted, 'Stand clear!' and fired.

'Carry him down to Mr Pierce,' said Hornblower,

indicating the injured man. 'Now let's see about these shot.'

Hornblower returned to Bush with a rueful look on his face, embarrassed and self-conscious.

'What's the trouble?' asked Bush.

'Those shot are too hot,' explained Hornblower. 'Damn it, I didn't think of that. They're half melted in the furnace and gone out of shape so that they won't fit the bore. What a fool I was not to think of that.'

As his superior officer, Bush did not admit that he had not thought of it either. He said nothing.

'And the ones that hadn't gone out of shape were too hot, anyway,' went on Hornblower. 'I'm the damndest fool God ever made. Mad as a hatter. Did you see how that gun went off? The men'll be scared now and won't lay their guns properly – too anxious to fire it off before the recoil catches them. God, I'm a careless son of a swab.'

'Easy, easy,' said Bush, a prey to conflicting emotions.

Hornblower pounding his left hand with his right fist as he upbraided himself was a comic sight; Bush could not help laughing at him. And Bush knew perfectly well that Hornblower had done excellently so far, really excellently, to have mastered at a moment's notice so much of the technique of using red-hot shot. Moreover, it must be confessed that Bush had experienced, during this expedition, more than one moment of pique at Hornblower's invariable bold assumption of responsibility; and the pique may even have been roused by a strong motive, jealousy at Hornblower's good management – an unworthy motive, which Bush would disclaim with shocked surprise if he became aware of it. Yet it made the sight of Hornblower's present discomfiture all the more amusing at the moment.

'Don't take on so,' said Bush with a grin.

'But it makes me wild to be such a –'

Hornblower cut the sentence off short. Bush could actually see him calling up his self-control and mastering himself, could see his annoyance at having been self-revelatory, could see the mask of the stoical and experienced fighting man put back into place to conceal the furious passions within.

'Would you take charge here, sir?' he said; it might be another person speaking. 'I'll go and take a look at the furnace, if I may. They'll have to go easy with those bellows.'

'Very good, Mr Hornblower. Send the ammunition up and I'll direct the fire on the schooner.'

'Aye aye, sir. I'll send up the last shot to go into the furnace. They won't be too hot yet, sir.'

Hornblower went darting down the ramp while Bush moved behind the guns to direct the fire. The fresh charges came up and were rammed home, the wet wads went in on top of the dry wads, and then the bearers began to arrive with the shot.

'Steady, all of you,' said Bush. 'These won't be as hot as the last batch. Take your aim carefully.'

But when Bush climbed on to the parapet and trained his telescope on the second schooner he could see that the schooner was changing her mind. She had brailed up her foresail and taken in her jibs; her boats were lying at an angle to her course, and were struggling, beetle-like, off her bows. They were pulling her round – she was going back up the bay and deciding not to run the gauntlet of the red-hot shot. There was the smouldering wreck of her consort to frighten her.

'She's turning tail!' said Bush loudly. 'Hit her while you can, you men.'

He saw the shot curving in the air, he saw the splashes in the water; he remembered how yesterday he had seen a ricochet shot from these very guns rebound from the water and strike the *Renown*'s massive side – one of the splashes was dead true for line, and might well indicate a hit.

'Fresh charges!' he bellowed, turning to make himself heard down at the magazine, 'Sponge out!'

But by the time the charges were in the guns the schooner had got her head right round, had reset her foresail, and was creeping back up the bay. Judging by the splashes of the last salvo she would be out of range before the next could be fired.

'Mr Hornblower!'

'Sir!'

''Vast sending any shot.'

'Aye aye, sir.'

When Hornblower came up again to the battery Bush pointed to the retreating schooner.

'He thought better of it, did he?' commented Hornblower. 'Yes, and those other two have anchored, I should say.'

His fingers were twitching for the one telescope again, and Bush handed it over.

'The other two aren't moving either,' said Hornblower, and then he swung round and trained the telescope down the bay towards the sea. '*Renown*'s gone about. She's caught the wind. Six miles? Seven miles? She'll be rounding the point in an hour.'

It was Bush's turn to grab for the telescope. There was no mistaking the trim of those topsails. From the *Renown* he transferred his attention to the opposite shore of the bay. There was the other battery with the Spanish flag above it – the flag was now drooping, now flapping lazily

in the light wind prevailing over the shore. He could make out no sign of activity whatever, and there was some finality in his gesture as he closed the telescope and looked at his second in command.

'Everything's quiet,' he said. 'Nothing to be done until *Renown* comes down.'

'That is so,' agreed Hornblower.

It was interesting to watch Hornblower's animation ebb away. Intense weariness was obvious in his face the moment he was off his guard.

'We can feed the men,' said Bush. 'And I'd like to have a look at the wounded. Those damned prisoners have to be sorted out – Whiting's got 'em all herded in the casemate, men and women, captains and drum boys. God knows what provisions there are here. We've got to see about that. Then we can set a watch, dismiss the watch below, and some of us can get some rest.'

'So we can,' said Hornblower; reminded of the necessary activities that still remained, he resumed his stolid expression. 'Shall I go down and start attending to it, sir?'

Prisoners in Revolt

With one of their forts captured, one ship burnt, and the others trapped in the bay, the Spaniards, under a flag of truce, offered to come to terms, but their demand for safe-conduct for their ships and men to the neighbouring Spanish island of Cuba in return for handing over everything intact without further fighting left Buckland in some doubt whether to accept. He would certainly be able to report that he had cleared the place of enemy shipping and demolished all the defences; moreover he could foresee difficulties in continuing the fighting. It would not be possible to take the second fort also by surprise and the three surviving privateers had fled up the bay into shallow water where the Renown could not follow.

Once again Hornblower came forward with a plan. This time his proposal was to land a gun from the ship under cover of darkness and hoist it up the steep cliffs which commanded the shallow end of the bay. He believed that the threat of sinking their ships at anchor would lead the Spaniards to see their position was hopeless and to surrender unconditionally. It was a daring and unusual scheme, but Buckland was persuaded to try it. After another night's toil, with sleep for nobody, the gun was hoisted high on the cliffs by daybreak next day. A few shots were enough for the Spaniards; they surrendered within the hour, and only the task of blowing up the forts remained to be done before leaving the scene of a most successful enterprise.

BUSH stood on the quarter-deck of the *Renown* at Buckland's side with his telescope trained on the fort.

'The party's leaving there now, sir,' he said; and then, after an interval, 'The boat's putting off from the landing-stage.'

The *Renown* swung at her anchor in the mouth of the Gulf of Samaná, and close beside her rode her three prizes. All four ships were jammed with the prisoners who had surrendered themselves, and sails were ready to loose the moment the *Renown* should give the signal.

'The boat's well clear now,' said Bush. 'I wonder – ah!'

The fort on the crest had burst into a great fountain of smoke, within which could be made out flying fragments of masonry. A moment later came the crash of the explosion. Two tons of gunpowder, ignited by the slow match left burning by the demolition party, did the work. Ramparts and bastions, tower and platform, all were dashed into ruins. Already at the foot of the steep slope to the water lay what was left of the guns, trunnions blasted off, muzzles split, and touchholes spiked; the other battery on the point across the water had already been blown up.

'It looks as if the damage is complete enough, sir,' said Bush.

'Yes,' said Buckland, his eye to his telescope observing the ruins as they began to show through the smoke and dust. 'We'll get under way as soon as the boat's hoisted in, if you please.'

'Aye aye, sir,' said Bush.

With the boat lowered on to its chocks the hands went to the capstan and hauled the ship laboriously up to her anchor; the sails were loosed as the anchor rose clear.

166

The main topsail aback gave her a trifle of sternway, and then, with the wheel hard over and hands at the headsail sheets, she came round. The topsails, braced up, caught the wind as the quartermaster at the wheel spun the spokes over hastily, and now she was under full command, moving easily through the water, heeling a little to the wind, the sea swinging under her cutwater, heading out close-hauled to weather Engano Point. Somebody forward began to cheer, and in a moment the entire crew was yelling lustily as the *Renown* left the scene of her victory. The prizes were getting under way at the same time, and the prize crews on board echoed the cheering. Bush's telescope could pick out Hornblower on the deck of *La Gaditana*, the big ship-rigged prize, waving his hat to the *Renown*.

'I'll see that everything is secure below, sir,' said Bush.

There were marine sentries beside the midshipmen's berth, bayonets fixed and muskets loaded. From within, as Bush listened, there was a wild babble of voices. Fifty women were cramped into that space, and almost as many children. That was bad, but it was necessary to confine them while the ship got under way. Later on they could be allowed on deck, in batches perhaps, for air and exercise. The hatchways in the lower gun-deck were closed by gratings, and every hatchway was guarded by a sentry. Up through the gratings rose the smell of humanity; there were four hundred Spanish soldiers confined down there in conditions not much better than prevailed in a slave ship. It was only since dawn that they had been down there, and already there was this stench. For the men, as for the women, there would have to be arrangements made to allow them to take the air in batches. It meant endless trouble and precaution;

Lieutenant Bush

Bush had already gone to considerable trouble to organize a system by which the prisoners should be supplied with food and drink. But every water butt was full, two boat-loads of yams had been brought on board from the shore, and, given the steady breeze that could be expected, the run to Kingston would be completed in less than a week. Then their troubles would be ended and the prisoners handed over to the military authorities – probably the prisoners would be as relieved as Bush would be.

On deck again Bush looked over at the green hills of Santo Domingo out on the starboard beam as, close-hauled, the *Renown* coasted along them; on that side, too, under her lee as his orders had dictated, Hornblower had the three prizes under easy sail. Even with this brisk seven-knot breeze blowing and the *Renown* with all sail set, those three vessels had the heels of her if they cared to show them; privateers depended both for catching their prey and evading their enemies on the ability to work fast to the windward, and Hornblower could soon have left the *Renown* far behind if he were not under orders to keep within sight and to leeward so that the *Renown* could run down to him and protect him if an enemy should appear. The prize crews were small enough in all conscience, and just as in the *Renown* Hornblower had all the prisoners he could guard battened down below.

Bush touched his hat to Buckland as the latter came on to the quarter-deck.

'I'll start bringing the prisoners up if I may, sir,' he said.

'Do as you think proper, if you please, Mr Bush.'

The quarter-deck for the women, the main deck for the men. It was hard to make them understand that they had to take turns; those of the women who were brought on deck seemed to fancy that they were going to be permanently separated from those kept below, and there was lamentation and expostulation which accorded ill with the dignified routine which should be observed on the quarter-deck of a ship of the line. And the children knew no discipline whatever, and ran shrieking about in all directions while harassed seamen tried to bring them back to their mothers. And other seamen had to be detailed to bring the prisoners their food and water.

Day by day the wind held fair; day by day the *Renown* surged along over the blue Caribbean with the prizes to leeward on the port bow; the prisoners, even the women, began to recover from their seasickness, and feeding them and guarding them became more and more matters of routine making less demand on everyone. They sighted Cape Beata to the northward and could haul their port tacks on board and lay a course direct for Kingston, but save for that they hardly had to handle a sail, for the wind blew steady and the hourly heaving of the log recorded eight knots with almost monotonous regularity. The sun rose splendidly behind them each morning; and each evening the bowsprit pointed into a flaming sunset. In the daytime the sun blazed down upon the ship save for the brief intervals when sharp rainstorms blotted out sun and sea; at night the ship rose and swooped with the following sea under a canopy of stars.

It was a dark, lovely night when Bush completed his evening rounds and went in to report to Buckland. The sentries were posted; the watch below was asleep with all lights out; the watch on deck had taken in the royals as a precaution against a rain squall striking the ship without warning in the darkness; the course was east by north and Mr Carberry had the watch, and the convoy was in sight a mile on the port bow. All this Bush recounted to Buckland in the time-honoured fashion of the navy, and Buckland listened to it with the navy's time-honoured patience.

'Thank you, Mr Bush.'

'Thank you, sir. Good night, sir.'

'Good night, Mr Bush.'

Bush's cabin opened on the half-deck; it was hot and stuffy with the heat in the tropics, but Bush did not care. He had six clear hours in which to sleep, seeing that he was going to take the morning watch, and he was not the man to waste any of that. He threw off his outer clothes, and standing in his shirt he cast a final look round his cabin before putting out the light. Shoes and trousers were on the sea-chest ready to be put on at a moment's notice in the event of an emergency. Sword and pistols were in their beckets against the bulkhead. All was well. The messenger who would come to call him would bring a lamp, so, using his hand to deflect his breath, he blew out the light. Then he dropped upon the cot, lying on his back with his arms and legs spread wide so as to allow the sweat every chance to evaporate, and he closed his eyes. Thanks to his blessed stolidity of temperament he was soon asleep. At midnight he awoke long enough to hear the watch called, and to tell himself blissfully that there was no need to awake, and he had not sweated enough to make his position on the cot uncomfortable.

Later he awoke again, and looked up into the darkness with uncomprehending eyes as his ears told him all was not well. There were loud cries, there was a rush of feet overhead. Perhaps a fluky rain squall had taken the ship aback. But those were the wrong noises. Were some of those cries cries of pain? Was that the scream of a woman? Were those infernal women squabbling with each other again? Now there was another rush of feet, and wild shouting, which brought Bush off his cot in a flash. He tore open his cabin door, and as he did so he heard the bang of a musket which left him in no doubt as to what was happening. He turned back and grabbed for sword and pistol, and by the time he was outside his cabin door again the ship was full of yelling tumult. It was as if the hatchways were the entrances to Hell, and pouring up through them were the infernal powers, screaming with triumph in the dimly lit recesses of the ship.

As he emerged the sentry under the lantern fired his musket, lantern and musket-flash illuminating a wave of humanity pouring upon the sentry and instantly submerging him; Bush caught a glimpse of a woman leading the wave, a handsome mulatto woman, wife to one of the privateer officers, now screaming with open mouth and staring eyes as she led the rush. Bush levelled his pistol and fired, but they were up to him in an instant. He

backed into his narrow doorway. Hands grabbed his
sword blade, and he tore it through their grip; he struck
wildly with his empty pistol, he kicked out with his bare
feet to free himself from the hands that grabbed at him.
Thrusting overhand with his sword he stabbed again
and again into the mass of bodies pressing against him.
Twice his head struck against the deck beams above, but
he did not feel the blows. Then the flood had washed
past him. There were shouts and screams and blows
farther along, but he himself had been passed by, saved
by the groaning men who wallowed at his feet – his bare
feet slipping in the hot blood that poured over them.

His first thought was for Buckland, but a single glance
aft assured him that by himself he stood no chance of
being of any aid to him, and in that case his post was on
the quarter-deck, and he ran out, sword in hand, to
make his way there. At the foot of the companion ladder
there was another whirl of yelling Spaniards; above there
were shouts and cries as the after guard fought it out.
Forward there was other fighting going on; the stars were
shining on white-shirted groups that fought and struggled
with savage desperation. Unknown to himself he was
yelling with the rest; a band of men turned upon him
as he approached, and he felt the heavy blow of a belaying
pin against his sword blade. But Bush inflamed with
fighting madness was an enemy to be feared; his immense
strength was allied to a lightfooted quickness. He struck
and parried, leaping over the cumbered deck. He knew
nothing, and during those mad minutes he thought of
nothing save to fight against these enemies, to reconquer
the ship by the strength of his single arm. Then he re-
gained some of his sanity at the moment when he struck
down one of the group against whom he was fighting.
He must rally the crew, set an example, concentrate

his men into a cohesive body. He raised his voice in a bellow.

'Renowns! Renowns! Here, Renowns! Come on!'

There was a fresh swirl in the mad confusion on the main deck. There was a searing pain across his shoulder-blade; instinctively he turned and his left hand seized a throat and he had a moment in which to brace himself and exert all his strength, with a wrench and a heave flinging the man on to the deck.

'Renowns!' he yelled again.

There was a rush of feet as a body of men rallied round him.

'Come on!'

But the charge that he led was met by a wall of men advancing forward against him from aft. Bush and his little group were swept back, across the deck, jammed against the bulwarks. Somebody shouted something in Spanish in front of him, and there was an eddy in the ring; then a musket flashed and banged. The flash lit up the swarthy faces that ringed them round, lit up the bayonet on the muzzle of the musket, and the man beside Bush gave a sharp cry and fell to the deck; Bush could feel him flapping and struggling against his feet. Someone at least had a firearm – taken from an arms rack or from a marine – and had managed to reload it. They would be shot to pieces where they stood, if they were to stand.

'Come on!' yelled Bush again, and sprang forward.

But the disheartened little group behind him did not stir, and Bush gave back from the rigid ring. Another musket flashed and banged, and another man fell. Someone raised his voice and called to them in Spanish. Bush could not understand the words, but he could guess it was a demand for surrender.

'I'll see you damned first!' he said.

He was almost weeping with rage. The thought of his magnificent ship falling into alien hands was appalling now that the realization of the possibility arose in his mind. A ship of the line captured and carried off into some Cuban port – what would England say? What would the navy say? He did not want to live to find out. He was a desperate man who wanted to die.

This time it was with no intelligible appeal to his men that he sprang forward, but with a wild animal cry; he was insane with fury, a fighting lunatic and with a lunatic's strength. He burst through the ring of his enemies, slashing and smiting, but he was the only one who succeeded; he was out on to the clear deck while the struggle went on behind him.

But the madness ebbed away. He found himself leaning – hiding himself, it might almost be said – beside one of the main deck eighteen-pounders, forgotten for the moment, his sword still in his hand, trying with a slow brain to take stock of his situation.

There were orders – Spanish orders – being shouted about the deck now. The ship had come up into the wind all aback when the quartermaster at the wheel had been overwhelmed, and she was wallowing in the trough of the waves, now coming up, now falling off again, with the canvas overhead all flapping and thundering. There were Spanish sea officers – those of the prizes – on board. They would be able to bring the ship under control in a few minutes. Even with a crew of landsmen they would be able to brace the yards, man the wheel, and set a course close-hauled up the Jamaica Channel. Beyond, only a long day's run, lay Santiago. Now there was the faintest, tiniest light in the sky. Morning – the awful morning – was about to break. Bush took a fresh grip on his sword hilt; his head was swimming and he passed his forearm over his face to wipe away the cobwebs that seemed to be gathering over his eyes.

And then, pale but silhouetted against the sky on the other side of the ship, he saw the topsail of another vessel moving slowly forward along the ship's side; masts, yards, rigging; another topsail slowly turning. There were wild shouts and yells from the *Renown*, a grinding crash as the two ships came together. An agonizing pause, like the moment before a roller breaks upon the shore. And then up over the bulwarks of the *Renown* appeared the heads and shoulders of men; the shakos of marines, the cold glitter of bayonets and cutlasses. There was Hornblower, hatless, swinging his leg over and leaping down to the deck, sword in hand, the others leaping with him on either hand. Weak and faint as he was, Bush still could think clearly enough to realize that Hornblower must have collected the prize crews from all three vessels before running alongside in the *Gaditana;* by Bush's calculations he could have brought thirty seamen and thirty marines to this attack. But while one part of Bush's brain could think with this clarity and logic the other part of it seemed to be hampered and clogged so that what went on before his eyes moved with nightmare slowness. It might have been a slow-order drill, as the boarding party climbed down on the deck. Everything was changed and unreal. The shouts of the Spaniards might have been the shrill cries of little children at play. Bush saw the muskets levelled and fired, but the irregular volley sounded in his ears no louder than popguns. The charge was sweeping the deck; Bush tried to spring forward to join with it but his legs, strangely, would not move. He found himself lying on the deck and his arms had no strength when he tried to lift himself up.

He saw the ferocious, bloody battle that was waged, a

fight as wild and as irregular as the one that had preceded it, when little groups of men seemed to appear from nowhere and fling themselves into the struggle, sometimes on this side and sometimes on that. Now came another surge of men, nearly naked seamen with Silk at their head; Silk was swinging the rammer of a gun, a vast, unwieldy weapon with which he struck out right and left at the Spaniards who broke before them. Another swirl and eddy in the fight; a Spanish soldier trying to run, limping, with a wounded thigh, and a British seaman with a boarding pike in pursuit, stabbing the wretched man under the ribs and leaving him moving feebly in the blood that poured from him.

Now the main deck was clear save for the corpses that lay heaped upon it, although below decks he could hear the fight going on, shots and screams and crashes. It all seemed to die away. This weakness was not exactly pleasant. To allow himself to put his head down on his arm and forget his responsibilities might seem tempting, but just over the horizon of his conscious mind there were hideous nightmare things waiting to spring out on him, of which he was frightened, but it made him weaker still to struggle against them. But his head was down on his arm, and it was a tremendous effort to lift it again; later it was a worse effort still, but he tried to force himself to make it, to rise and deal with all the things that must be done. Now there was a hard voice speaking, painful to his ears.

'This 'ere's Mr Bush, sir. 'Ere 'e is!'

Hands were lifting his head. The sunshine was agonizing as it poured into his eyes, and he closed his eyelids tight to keep it out.

'Bush! Bush!' That was Hornblower's voice, pleading and tender. 'Bush, please, speak to me.'

Two gentle hands were holding his face between them. Bush could just separate his eyelids sufficiently to see Hornblower bending over him, but to speak called for more strength than he possessed. He could only shake his head a little, smiling because of the sense of comfort and security conveyed by Hornblower's hands.

The Court of Inquiry

When the Renown *reached Kingston, Bush was sent ashore to the naval hospital, for he was still very weak from his wounds. As they took him up on deck in a stretcher he caught a glimpse of Captain Cogshill coming aboard to assume command of the ship. Captain Sawyer was dead; he had been murdered on his sickbed by the Spaniards during their attempt to capture the* Renown, *and the admiral had appointed Cogshill to replace him. The admiral had also ordered a court of inquiry and nominated Cogshill to serve as one of its members, but several days passed before Bush was well enough to attend and give evidence.*

THE court of inquiry was not nearly as awe-inspiring as a court-martial. There was no gun fired, no court-martial flag hoisted; the captains who constituted the board wore their everyday uniforms, and the witnesses were not required to give their evidence under oath; Bush had forgotten about this last fact until he was called into the court.

'Please take a seat, Mr Bush,' said the president. 'I understand you are still weak from your wounds.'

Bush hobbled across to the chair indicated and was just able to reach it in time to sit down. The great cabin of the *Renown* was sweltering hot. The president had the log-book and journal in front of him, and he held in his hand what Bush recognized to be his own report regarding the attack on Samaná, which he had addressed to Buckland.

'This report of yours does you credit, Mr Bush,' said the president. 'It appears that you stormed this fort with no more than six casualties, although it was constructed with a ditch, parapets, and ramparts in regular style, and defended by a garrison of seventy men, and armed with twenty-four-pounders.'

'We took them by surprise, sir,' said Bush.

'It is that which is to your credit.'

The surprise of the garrison of Samaná could not have been greater than Bush's own surprise at this reception; he was expecting something far more unpleasant and inquisitorial. A glance across at Buckland, who had been called in before him, was not quite so reassuring; Buckland was pale and unhappy. But there was something he must say before the thought of Buckland should distract him.

'The credit should be given to Lieutenant Hornblower, sir,' he said. 'It was his plan.'

'So you very handsomely say in your report. I may as well say at once that it is the opinion of this court that all the circumstances regarding the attack on Samaná and the subsequent capitulation are in accordance with the best traditions of the service.'

'Thank you, sir.'

'Now we come to the next matter. The attempt of the prisoners to capture the *Renown*. You were by this time acting as first lieutenant of the ship, Mr Bush?'

'Yes, sir.'

Step by step Bush was taken through the events of that night. He was responsible under Buckland for the arrangements made for guarding and feeding the prisoners. There were fifty women, wives of the prisoners, under guard in the midshipmen's berth. Yes, it was difficult to supervise them as closely as the men. Yes, he had gone his rounds after pipedown. Yes, he had heard a disturbance. And so on.

'And you were found lying among the dead, unconscious from your wounds?'

'Yes, sir.'

'Thank you, Mr Bush.'

'I don't expect any of you gentlemen wish to ask Mr Bush any more questions?' asked the president of the court in such a way that questions could not possibly have been asked. 'Call Lieutenant Hornblower.'

Hornblower made his bow to the court; he was wearing that impassive expression which Bush knew by now to conceal an internal turbulence. He was asked as few questions on Samaná as Bush had been.

'It has been suggested,' said the president, 'that this attack on the fort, and the hoisting up of the gun to search the bay, were on your initiative?'

'I can't think why that suggestion was made, sir. Mr Buckland bore the entire responsibility.'

'I won't press you further about that, Mr Hornblower, then. I think we all understand. Now, let us hear about your recapture of the *Renown*. What first attracted your attention?'

It called for steady questioning to get the story out of Hornblower. He had heard a couple of musket shots, which had worried him, and then he saw the *Renown* come up into the wind, which made him certain something was seriously wrong. So he had collected his prize crews together and laid the *Renown* on board.

'Were you not afraid of losing the prizes, Mr Hornblower?'

'Better to lose the prizes than the ship, sir. Besides –'

'Besides what, Mr Hornblower?'

'I had every sheet and halliard cut in the prizes before we left them, sir. It took them some time to reeve new ones, so it was easy to recapture them.'

'You seem to have thought of everything, Mr Hornblower,' said the president, and there was a buzz of

approval through the court. 'And you seem to have made a very prompt counter-attack on the *Renown*. You did not wait to ascertain the extent of the danger? Yet for all you knew the attempt to take the ship might have already failed.'

'In that case no harm was done except the disabling of the rigging of the prizes, sir. But if the ship had actually fallen into the hands of the prisoners it was essential that an attack should be directed on her before any defence could be organized.'

'We understand. Thank you, Mr Hornblower.'

The inquiry was nearly over. Carberry was still too ill with his wounds to be able to give evidence; Whiting of the marines was dead. The court conferred only a moment before announcing its findings.

'It is the opinion of this court,' announced the president, 'that strict inquiry should be made among the Spanish prisoners to determine who it was that murdered Captain Sawyer, and that the murderer, if still alive, should be brought to justice. And as the result of our examination of the surviving officers of H.M.S. *Renown* it is our opinion that no further action is necessary.'

That meant there would be no court-martial. Bush found himself grinning with relief as he sought to meet Hornblower's eye, but when he succeeded his smile met with a cold reception. Bush tried to shut off his smile and look like a man of such clear conscience that it was no relief to be told that he would not be court-martialled. And a glance at Buckland changed his elation to a feeling of pity. The man was desperately unhappy; his professional ambitions had come to an abrupt end. After the capitulation of Samaná he must have cherished hope, for with that considerable achievement to his credit, and his captain unfit for service, there was every possibility that he would receive the vital promotion to commander at least, possibly even to captain. The fact that he had been surprised in bed when the Spanish prisoners captured the *Renown* and had been able to do nothing to defend his ship meant an end to all that. He would always be remembered for it, and the fact would remain in people's minds when the circumstances were forgotten. He was doomed to remain an ageing lieutenant.

Bush remembered guiltily that it was only by good fortune that he himself had awakened in time. His wounds might be painful, but they had served an invaluable purpose in diverting attention from his own responsibility; he had fought until he had fallen unconscious, and perhaps that was to his credit, but Buckland would have done the same had the opportunity been granted him. But Buckland was damned, while he himself had come through the ordeal at least no worse off than he had been before. Good luck came and went in the navy as unpredictably as death chose its victims when a broadside swept a crowded deck.

'Ah, Mr Bush,' said Captain Cogshill, 'it's a pleasure to see you on your feet. I hope you will remain on board to dine with me. I hope to secure the presence of the other lieutenants.'

'With much pleasure, sir,' said Bush. Every lieutenant said that in reply to his captain's invitation.

Captain Cogshill was a courtly host. There were flowers in the great cabin now; they must have been kept hidden away in his sleeping cabin while the inquiry was being held so as not to detract from the formality of the proceedings. And the cabin windows were wide open, and a wind scoop brought into the cabin what little air was moving.

'That is a land-crab salad before you, Mr Hornblower. Coconut-fed land crab. Some prefer it to dairy-fed pork. Perhaps you will serve it to those who would care for some?'

The steward brought in a vast smoking joint which he put on the table.

'A saddle of fresh lamb,' said the captain. 'Sheep do badly in these islands and I fear this may not be fit to eat. But perhaps you will at least try it. Mr Buckland, will you carve? You see, gentlemen, I still have some real potatoes left – one grows weary of yams. Mr Hornblower, will you take wine?'

'With pleasure, sir.'

'And Mr Bush – to your speedy recovery, sir.'

Bush drained his glass thirstily. The surgeon had

warned him, when he left the hospital, that over-indulgence in spirituous liquors might result in inflammation of his wounds, but there was pleasure in pouring the wine down his throat and feeling the grateful warmth it brought to his stomach. The dinner proceeded.

'You gentlemen who have served on this station before must be acquainted with this,' said the captain, contemplating a steaming dish that had been laid before him. 'A West Indian pepper pot – not as good as one finds in Trinidad, I fear. Mr Hornblower, will you make your first essay? Come in!'

The last words were in response to a knock on the cabin door. A smartly dressed midshipman entered. His beautiful uniform, his elegant bearing, marked him as one of that class of naval officer in receipt of a comfortable allowance from home, or even of substantial means of his own. Some sprig of the nobility, doubtless, serving his legal time until favouritism and interest should whisk him up the ladder of promotion.

'I'm sent by the admiral, sir,' he announced.

Of course. Bush, his perceptions comfortably sensitized with wine, could see at once that with those clothes and that manner he must be on the admiral's staff.

'And what's your message?' asked Cogshill.

'The admiral's compliments, sir, and he'd like Mr Hornblower's presence on board the flagship as soon as is convenient.'

'And dinner not half-way finished,' commented Cogshill, looking at Hornblower. But an admiral's request for something as soon as convenient meant immediately, convenient or not. Very likely it was a matter of no importance, either.

'I'd better leave, sir, if I may,' said Hornblower. He glanced at Buckland. 'May I have a boat, sir?'

'Pardon me, sir,' interposed the midshipman. 'The admiral said that the boat which brought me would serve to convey you to the flagship.'

'That settles it,' said Cogshill. 'You'd better go, Mr Hornblower. We'll save some of this pepper pot for you against your return.'

'Thank you, sir,' said Hornblower, rising.

As soon as he had left, the captain asked the inevitable question.

'What in the world does the admiral want with Hornblower?'

He looked round the table and received no verbal reply. There was a strained look on Buckland's face, however, as Bush saw. It seemed as if in his misery Buckland was clairvoyant.

'Well, we'll know in time,' said Cogshill. 'The wine's beside you, Mr Buckland. Don't let it stagnate.'

Dinner went on. The pepper pot rasped on Bush's palate and inflamed his stomach, making the wine doubly grateful when he drank it. When the cheese was removed, and the cloth with it, the steward brought in fruit and nuts in silver dishes.

'Port,' said Captain Cogshill. ''79. A good year. About this brandy I know little, as one might expect in these times.'

Brandy could only come from France, smuggled, presumably, and as a result of trading with the enemy.

'But here,' went on the captain, 'is some excellent Dutch geneva – I bought it at the prize sale after we took St Eustatius. And here is another Dutch liquor – it comes from Curaçao, and if the orange flavour is not too sickly for your palates you might find it pleasant. Swedish schnapps, fiery but excellent, I fancy – that was after we captured Saba. The wise man does not mix grain and grape, so they say, but I understand schnapps is made from potatoes, and so does not come under the ban. Mr Buckland?'

'Schnapps for me,' said Buckland a little thickly.

'Mr Bush?'

'I'll drink along with you, sir.'

That was the easiest way of deciding.

'Then let us make it brandy. Gentlemen, may Boney grow bonier than ever.'

They drank the toast, and the brandy went down to warm Bush's interior to a really comfortable pitch. He was feeling happy and relaxed, and two toasts later he was feeling better than he had felt since the *Renown* left Plymouth.

'Come in!' said the captain.

The door opened slowly, and Hornblower stood framed in the opening. There was the old look of strain in his face; Bush could see it even though Hornblower's figure seemed to waver a little before his eyes – the way objects appeared over the rack of red-hot cannon balls at Samaná – and although Hornblower's countenance seemed to be a little fuzzy round the edges.

'Come, in, come in, man,' said the captain. 'The toasts are just beginning. Sit in your old place. Brandy for heroes, as Johnson said in his wisdom. Mr Bush!'

'V-victorious war. O-oceans of gore. P-prizes galore. B-b-beauty ashore. Hic,' said Bush, inordinately proud of himself that he had remembered that toast and had it ready when called upon.

'Drink fair, Mr Hornblower,' said the captain, 'we have a start of you already. A stern chase is a long chase.'

Hornblower put his glass to his lips again.

'Mr Buckland!'

'Jollity and – jollity and – jollity and – and – and –

mirth,' said Buckland, managing to get the last word out at last. His face was as red as a beetroot and seemed to Bush's heated imagination to fill the entire cabin like the setting sun; most amusing.

'You've come back from the admiral, Mr Hornblower,' said the captain with sudden recollection.

'Yes, sir.'

The curt reply seemed out of place in the general atmosphere of goodwill; Bush was distinctly conscious of it, and of the pause which followed.

'Is all well?' asked the captain at length, apologetic about prying into someone else's business and yet led to do so by the silence.

'Yes, sir.' Hornblower was turning his glass round and round on the table between the long, nervous fingers, every finger a foot long, it seemed to Bush. 'He has made me commander into *Retribution*.'

The words were spoken quietly, but they had the impact of pistol shots in the silence of the room, for they meant that Hornblower had been selected for promotion over the heads of both Buckland and Bush.

'God bless my soul!' said the captain. 'Then that's our new toast. To the new commander, and a cheer for him, too!'

Bush cheered lustily and downed his brandy.

'Good old Hornblower!' he said. 'Good old Hornblower!'

To him it was really excellent news; he leaned over and patted Hornblower's shoulder. He knew his face was one big smile, and he put his head on one side and his shoulder on the table so that Hornblower should get the full benefit of it.

Buckland put his glass down on the table with a sharp tap.

'Damn you!' he said. 'Damn you! Damn you to Hell!'

'Easy there!' said the captain hastily. 'Let's fill the glasses. A brimmer there, Mr Buckland. Now, our country! Noble England! Queen of the waves!'

Buckland's anger was drowned in the fresh flood of liquor, yet later in the session his sorrows overcame him and he sat at the table weeping quietly, with the tears running down his cheeks; but Bush was too happy to allow Buckland's misery to affect him. He always remembered that afternoon as one of the most successful dinners he had ever attended. He could also remember Hornblower's smile at the end of dinner.

'We can't send you back to the hospital today,' said Hornblower. 'You'd better sleep in your own cot tonight. Let me take you there.'

That was very agreeable. Bush put both arms round Hornblower's shoulders and walked with dragging feet. It did not matter that his feet dragged and his legs would not function while he had this support; Hornblower was the best man in the world and Bush could announce it by singing 'For He's a Jolly Good Fellow', while lurching along the alleyway. He was a little astonished that the ship should sway like this while at anchor.

Some other Puffin Classics

Roger Lancelyn Green	Adventures of Robin Hood
Jack London	The Call of the Wild White Fang
George MacDonald	At the Back of the North Wind The Princess and Curdie The Princess and the Goblin
Captain Marryat	The Children of the New Forest
E. Nesbit	The Enchanted Castle Five Children and It The Last of the Dragons The Phoenix and the Carpet The Wouldbegoods The Railway Children
Eleanor H. Porter	Pollyanna Pollyanna Grows Up
H. Rider Haggard	King Solomon's Mines
Anna Sewell	Black Beauty
Johanna Spyri	Heidi
R. L. Stevenson	Kidnapped Dr Jekyll and Mr Hyde Treasure Island
Bram Stoker	Dracula
Mark Twain	Adventures of Huckleberry Finn Adventures of Tom Sawyer The Prince and the Pauper
Jules Verne	Journey to the Centre of the Earth
Kate Douglas Wiggins	Rebecca of Sunnybrook Farm
Oscar Wilde	The Happy Prince and Other Stories